TULLIE SUMMERS

Wake Up

Contents

Chapter 1

Mason
April - Kindergarten

Peach lips stretch into a huge grin revealing perfectly straight, square baby teeth amongst heavily freckled cheeks that are only a little pinker than the crayon Milo is using to draw a picture of Elsie. I don't mind that Milo is always the one who makes her smile like that as long as she keeps doing it.

"Okay…almost there," Milo has his tongue slightly stuck out as he concentrates on trying to make sure it is a perfect copy of Elsie. I know it won't be that great, Milo isn't a real artist but she'll like it anyway. She likes to keep all the presents we make her in a box at home that she puts under her bed. She calls it her remember me box.

I laughed when I first heard her say it and corrected her that it was a 'memory box'. My parents had some so I knew what it was supposed to be called. She insisted it was a 'remember me' box though and we had argued so much about it that her dad sent me home while Milo got to stay and play. I went back the next day to say sorry and she'd given me the best hug ever, but I wasn't allowed to see or talk about her memory box anymore. Fair trade I guess.

"Done!" Milo holds up the drawing proudly and I scoff. It is worse than I thought it'd be. Just a couple of blobs that barely look like a person - I mean come on who has only one gigantic arm like that?

"What is that?!" I laugh. We are about to be first graders, he really needs to step his game up. He rolls his eyes at me and starts slowly pointing out the different features of his disaster like I'm just blind or something.

"…and these are her big green eyes!" Milo defends his work, clearly frustrated I pointed out any flaws. Again. This is the usual and right on cue Elsie pipes in.

"Well, I like it! I think it is perfect and I'm going to put it in my remember me box." She plucks it from Milo's hand and turns that super cute smile on me. "Are you coming over after school today, Mason?" Hope fills her eyes and I hate knowing I'm disappointing her again.

"I can't. My dad needs me for stuff." I say with a shrug like it doesn't really matter.

"But you haven't been over all week!" She whines.

"Yeah, what's your dad need you for anyway?" Milo chimes in, equally disappointed I can't come over. We used to hang out everyday before, during and after school - even on the weekends. See, we all ride the same bus because Elsie's house is right next to mine and her house is right next to Milo's. Since she lives in the middle we decided her house was the best place to hang around - plus she has the best snacks. But my dads been home from deployment for a week now and I haven't been allowed to go anywhere.

"I know! It's just stuff, okay?" I shrug again. I don't really know how to explain the things my dad has been making me do since he got back. He isn't even acting like my dad anymore. Besides, he told me not to tell anyone. Something about not being able to tell who your real enemies were or whatever. I think Elsie knows I'm not telling them everything because she is staring real hard at me like my mom does sometimes. "Stop staring at me." I grumble at her as the last bell rings and Mr. Rhea dismisses us for the day.

I speed walk to the bus to get a moment to myself. Deep down I have this feeling I should tell someone what is happening, that it isn't normal to have to 'sweep' the house for 'bugs'. Like spy stuff. Dad thinks maybe Milo's parents are bad guys but he also seems to think that about the old lady across the street.

Last night, he had me outside in the thunderstorm running and doing push-ups and stuff because he says I need to be ready. But ready for what I don't know. Mom stood by the back door and cried, I tried to tell her I was fine but she wouldn't listen. Dad got so mad that he eventually shoved her inside and closed the blinds. I knew she was watching from their bedroom after that though.

"Hey," Elsie pants as she catches up. "I'm sorry. I know you can't do anything about it. It's your dad." She shrugs and smiles as we board the bus. She sits between me and Milo on the bus, just like how our houses are.

"Yeah…" I almost start to mention that my dad is acting weird but Milo plops down into his seat and I swallow my confession. I like Milo but I'm not sure we'd be close friends without Elsie in the mix.

"You two left me! Not cool!" He fumes while scrunching up his face at me.

"We were all going to meet up fast anyway. We're neighbors." Elsie shrugs again as she pats his head. His cheeks turn a dark red and I shake my head at him. Milo says he loves Elsie but my mom says we are all too young to know what love is.

They chatter about their afternoon plans and whose house to have dinner at tonight while I glower out the window. I had missed my dad when he was away but now I kind of wish he hadn't come back. Guilt settles on my shoulders at that thought. The bus ride is short as usual but the cop cars, fire trucks and ambulances on our street are not. The three of us clammer to get off the bus only to be stopped by Milo's mom.

Her face is all red and blotchy as she addresses the bus driver in low tones. Milo inches closer to try and hear over all the sirens. I feel like my heart is going to burst out of my body and I might throw up like that time I ate 6 hot dogs to try and impress Elsie. His mom steps off the bus and we hurry to follow.

There is yellow tape surrounding my yard and so many people in uniforms. Elsie holds my hand and I look at Milo confused. He grabs my other hand and I know for sure something bad has happened because he is crying now too and Milo doesn't cry a lot.

"Mason, you're going to come stay with us for a little while okay?" His mom kneels down in front of me and grips my shoulders like I'll need to be held up. "Mason, buddy."Her voice cracks and she closes her eyes taking big breaths.

"I want my mom!" I declare, shaking. Something horrible has happened, why isn't my mom here?

"She's gone. Your dad won't be around for a long

time either."

Chapter 2

Mason
April - Seventh Grade

S huffling my boots on the tiled floor I wait for Elsie to get out of class. No doubt Milo has filled her in on the little trades I'd been making during gym class. So what, it is just a little weed. A way to make money and, hey, if a girl wants it badly enough and can't pay with cash, who am I to judge their other offerings?

Milo is just jealous cause he can't even get the one girl he has been obsessed with for years to see him as anything but a friend and I've got girls lining up to suck me off. I bet he hasn't even seen a boob yet, what a nerd.

Still, he'd done me a solid by not reporting me to the principal or worse his mom. I know Elsie won't tell on me either. Milo is too much of a wuss and for some reason Elsie still likes having me around. Maybe Milo didn't say anything just because Elsie would be pissed at him if he did. Doesn't matter either way, long as I keep getting to make cash and they stay out of the way, everything will be fine.

Nerves bounce around my stomach as I wait though. Much as I wish I could stop caring, Elsie's opinion of me matters for some reason. The bell rings and I settle against the lockers, putting on my best I-don't-care face.

Milo finds me first. He didn't start puberty when I did and he still looks like the gangly little kid he's always been. Metal framed glasses and youthful roundness making him the golden-boy, baby-faced wonder. *Gag.* He even sports light blue eyes and gold blonde hair that he has recently started to style instead of side comb. In comparison, I am like a foot taller and look more akin to the high schoolers that supply my weed than I do Milo. Torn jeans, hand me down band shirts and hoodies are more my style than the polos Milo likes to wear. We may have grown up in the same house since my dad went off his rocker and killed my mom but we can't be more different.

Elsie materializes out of thin air while I assess how much Milo cramps my style these days. Her strawberry blonde hair is pulled into a too-tight bun again today and she looks like she hasn't slept a wink. She chews on her bottom lip and anxiety practically rolls off her. I grab the back of my neck looking down at her, is it really worth it to worry her like this?

"So you're selling weed now?" She asks quietly, no judgment in her voice. She just wants to hear it from me I guess.

"Yeah." I shrug, trying to play it cool. She purses her lips as she studies me for a long second.

"Okay," she exhales heavily and gives me a tired smile, "I gotta get to class. See you on the bus." Milo sputters as we both watch her walk away.

"That's it?! No lecture, nothing?!" He flails his arms about wildly and some of our peers start to stare at him.

"Knock it off, man. She said it's fine." I push past him and head towards my own class for the end of the day. I don't turn to see him huff and puff because clearly he is the only one willing to say anything about my questionable choices. Maybe she doesn't care as much as either of us thought after all.

Taking my seat in the back of my history class I don't bother pulling out materials like the other kids do. There isn't any point, I'm not going to use any of this stuff when I get older anyway. Plus, I have a photographic memory so I know I'll pass all my classes. Kelley turns all the way around in her desk to face me with a flirty smile. I like Kelley, she has pretty black hair and olive skin and she lets me look at her notes before tests.

"Hey Mason, I heard you might want to meet at the playhouse later?" She bites her lip and leans on to my desk so I can see down her shirt. Ah yes, the main reason I like Kelley, she had hit puberty at the end of fifth grade and is well on her way to being a full on woman with the curves to prove it.

"I could be persuaded." I smirk. The play house is a literal children's play house in Garters back yard. It's where we get together to smoke and feel up on each other without any adults seeing. Garter's mom works a lot so she is never home and his dad isn't in the picture so it works out perfectly.

"Oh really," She flutters her eyelashes at me. "and what would I have to do to get you to ditch your tagalongs so we can do some exploring, hmm?" Just as I started to get excited, she had to go and ruin it.

"Tagalongs?" I echo as the smirk falls off my face. If she notices the change in my mood, she isn't bright enough to stop digging the hole deeper.

"You know, Milo and - god what's her name?" She taps her finger to her chin and makes a show of pretending to think on it. " I guess it doesn't really matter since you won't remember it either when I'm done blowing your mind." She grins at me and runs her tongue over her teeth in a move I think was supposed to be sexy but is just kind of weird.

Anger simmers in my chest. Sure, Milo is a pain in my ass but he is also basically my brother. And

Elsie is worth so much more than a blow job in a play house. I don't know why Elsie gets bullied by the other girls but it sure does grind my gears.

"I'd like to see you try, Elsie is hard to forget." I smile at Kelley trying to hide the malice in my voice. She smirks right back, clearly rising to the challenge. She winks at me and spins to face the front. She'll be pissed at me tomorrow for standing her up but for some reason letting her choke on my dick feels wrong if she is going to be mean and degrading to Elsie. Everyone knows me, Milo and Elsie are best friends and have been since the first day of kindergarten. Well, except my weed suppliers and their friends anyway. I don't want them anywhere near Milo and Elsie.

Class flys by and I haul ass to the bus loop. Now that we are older and bigger only one of us gets to sit by Elsie on the bus. Today, I need it to be me. I need her closeness to confirm that she isn't mad at me for my side business and I need to know nothing is going to change. I'm a damned sucker for Elsie no matter how much I wish I wasn't.

Sliding into our usual seat on the bus, I wait for my best friends to join me. Staring intently out the window I scan the parking lot for them as the bus begins to fill with other students. We don't have a huge class, maybe two hundred kids attend the middle school in total. As the seconds pass I start to worry maybe I forgot something when I don't see that familiar streak of strawberry hair. Milo climbs on the bus but doesn't sit which only bewilders me more.

"Come on. I'll get mom to pick us up, Elsie isn't taking the bus today." He says matter of factly. Far too serious for her to just be staying after school for a club or something. I don't ask any questions as we both exit the bus. At some point, it became a habit where if one of us didn't ride the bus then none of us did.

"What's wrong?" I demand, it coming out harsher than I'd intended it to.

"I'm not really sure, she doesn't want to go home." He shrugs and fidgets nervously with his backpack strap. We round the corner of the building to the back side of the school where Elsie is sitting on the grass with her back to the bricks. We each sit on either side of her and wait for her to say something.

"What's going on Elsie?" I ask gently after a few minutes of tense silence.

"My mom doesn't want me hanging out with you anymore, Mason." She starts crying and I put my arm around her shoulders. It isn't the first time her mom has made it known she doesn't like me very much. "S-she thinks we're going to … you know…" she gestures wildly, her eyes bugging out of her head as she blushes.

"Do it?" Asks Milo oh-so-helpfully.

"Nah shit dumb ass!" I glare at him and he holds his hands up in surrender.

"Anyway, she keeps trying to push for me to date Milo because apparently then I'll be trustworthy?!" She huffs at the ridiculousness. Milo blushes and looks away clearly uncomfortable. If it wasn't for the adults meddling, they might have already been together but everytime one of their moms suggests they'd make a good couple Elsie stomps the brakes and reminds EVERYONE that the three of us are just friends. "Even worse, she doesn't even see how hard I've been studying - doesn't care! She texted me that I needed to chill out since I'll just be a trophy wife someday anyway!" She angry sobs and with a lack of words I decide her mom is right about one thing - she needed to chill out. Carefully, I pull her hair down and massage her scalp.

"You know…maybe your mom has a point. It's only middle school, El. You're way too stressed out." Milo suggests like an absolute idiot as soon as her sobs start to actually calm down.

"It matters Milo! I want to go to an Ivy League college, so, yes it freaking matters!" She stands knocking my hand away as she all but yells at him. She has been a lot more irritable lately and the gears in my mind start spinning faster and faster. A stain is in an odd spot on the back of her hoodie that she had wrapped around her waist.

"Okay, okay. You're right. I'm sorry." Milo placates, not at all picking up on the shift I am sensing. Not wanting to embarrass her I stand and lean in to whisper in her ear.

"Elsie, you're bleeding, babe." I lean back to scan her horrified face as her hands fly to cover her backside.

"Oh my god." She exclaims and starts sobbing again. *Shit.* I take my hoodie off and secure it around her waist to hide the stained one while Milo stares up at me from the ground looking completely confused.

"Call your mom, tell her to bring Elsie some clothes and girl stuff." I order and thank the gods when he doesn't question it, whipping out his phone and dialing.

We wait the next 20 minutes or so awkwardly as I hold a crying El and Milo tries to pretend he hasn't caught on to the fact Elsie is on her period and that is probably why she has been acting kind of weird lately.

When Milo's mom finally rounds the corner and takes in the scene she doesn't break her stride. His mom is a tall woman, resembling a Barbie but with a permanent scowl these days and I often wonder if she regrets taking me in.

"Elsie, I brought you some clothes and pads. I

also called your parents and let them know why you missed the bus. Let's get in my car and you can clean up at the gas station over there." We all nod quietly and follow her back to the car. When we get to the gas station his mom goes inside with El while we wait in the back seat.

"So. She is a woman now, right?" Milo asks.

"Yup." I pop the 'p' loudly and cross my arms.

"Does this…change anything?" he asks, god he sounds like a little kid.

"I dunno dude, depends on her. She could turn into a raging bitch." I deadpan with a shrug.

Chapter 3

Mason
November - Junior year

"Elsie, baby, please wait!" Jett chases after Elsie as she flees from his house to my car. My matte black, bought it with coke-cash-camaro that has her name embroidered on the passenger seat. She holds her blouse closed with one hand and throws open the door with the other wasting no time slamming it shut. I hit the lock button and rev my engine so the douche will back off, I don't need a hit and run charge while I am on probation. Once he jumps back like the bottom feeding bitch he is, I peel away with tires screeching.

I want to go back and beat his face in. Or set his house on fire like I had that guy Matteo's place six months ago when he didn't get the message that she wasn't there to do anything but study. I also kind of want to put her over my knee and paddle her ass for her poor taste in men.

"What'd he do?" Milo asks from the back seat, sounding every bit as pissed as I am.

"Thanks for picking me up." Elsie has started avoiding answering questions when it comes to Jett, her on again off again boyfriend from the last year or so. He had been a bad decision when her dad walked out on her mom and for some reason she keeps going back to him even though it always ends with her in tears and me in cuffs.

"Answer the damn question or I'm leaving you on the curb." I glower at her as I pull over. Her hair is a thick curtain between us, guarding her from my searching gaze. Something tingles my spidey senses cause she almost never hides from me or Milo. I snatch her hair back out of the way roughly and swear as I raged against my steering wheel pummeling into the damned thing until it bends at the top. One more thing I gotta fucking fix now, damn it.

"What?!" Milo demands,trying to get a look at her face. She covers her busted lip and the blooming bruise on her jaw with her hand as she sends daggers at me.

"Fucking show him!" I gesture grandly at Milo. I am going to jail, I am going to murder Jett Starkal. She stares at me with tears in her eyes as she drops her hand. Milo gently turns her face with his finger and I want to snap it off his hand. Fucking stupid patient ass gentle ass...

We aren't the kids we used to be. Now, Milo is the perfect rendition of a Ken doll and has seemingly never ending patience. It is infuriating. He never gets mad, gets in trouble or makes Elsie angry like I do. He is funny and charming and handsome according to the girls at school but to me he is just a pain in the ass. Mainly because I know he is better for El than I am and I fucking hate that.

I might be a pot-headed drug-dealing no-good drop out but hey at least I have a cool car, good looks and a steady flow of cash to help make sure my girl is taken care of. Of course, it'd help if she would just date the idiot in my backseat and stop messing around with the other guys that all the adults in this town seem to hate.

"Go back." Milo orders in an odd turn of events. I turned and stared at him in shock, catching sight of Elsie's bruised jaw dropping at the same time. I recover faster than she does though and pull a very illegal U-turn. Hell yeah, we are gonna go fuck some shit up. Maybe Milo isn't so perfect after all.

"NO! STOP THE CAR! STOP IT RIGHT NOW!" Elsie yells, she is angry and hurt and panicking. She tugs my arm like that will stop me. I grab her wrist and pin it to her lap, driving with one hand. "Please." Her broken whisper has all my rage evaporating in the blink of an eye and I ease off the gas.

"No, I am tired of you letting men hurt you." Milo growls. "You are done dating. If you can't pick a decent guy then you shouldn't be dating at all." He sounds like her dad, not her friend and definitely not the guy who wants to be the one dating her.

I half watch her out of the side of my eye, waiting for her to lash out at him like she does with me when I try to tell her what to do. She has grown into a beautiful young woman. She stopped getting taller sometime in middle school, leaving her at about five foot but her body had been busy putting effort into growing her some curves apparently. Everything about Elsie is soft and, aside from when it is just us, she has gotten a lot quieter too. She has perfected a standard make up look of gloss and mascara, her hair hangs in loose waves and she always seemed to be wearing soft, muted colors that are in high contrast to my almost all black wardrobe and Milo's edgy business aesthetic.

"I don't want Mason to get arrested again." She states quietly. She hasn't agreed to Milo's outburst but she doesn't yell at him like she would've with me. I sigh and slow the car even more. Of course she is worried about me. Elsie is always worried about me. I can't even blame her either because I give her every reason to worry.

I've wrecked more cars than I care to count, regularly break the law and semi regularly get arrested for it. I had been given probation about a month ago for arson and the judge warned me it was my last chance. If I get put in those shiny bracelets again, I'll be facing adult charges.

"Let's just get some food and ice for your face." I decided as I wiped a tear from her cheek. She bobs her head rapidly and swipes at the remaining tears.

"So this is the one time you are just gonna let it go huh?" Milo taunts from the back seat as he scoffs and throws himself backwards.

"Mi, please don't. You know there's better options than both of y'all getting in trouble with the law. It's not even that bad." Elsie turns to face him as she pleads for him to drop it.

"Not even that bad?! El do you hear yourself? He - he... how exactly did you get hurt?" He is losing steam fast and suddenly realized we don't even know what happened yet. I don't really care, I'll make sure he pays for whatever happened and I won't get caught this time.

"He ... It doesn't matter." She sighs as she finally starts fixing her shirt. She is right, it doesn't matter because Jett will pay. Any time she isn't returned to me in the same condition I drop her off in I make sure someone pays the toll. Milo blows out a deep breath and nods, I guess he knows without my backup there is no way he can do anything about it.

I pull through the drive through of Pop's Burgers

and order our regular plus a cup of ice. My phone buzzes as we wait and I skim the text : drop @8.

Great, I'll have to drop them off and hit up my place before meeting Bullet. I'd moved out at 16 last year and El's mom had co-signed on an apartment for me. She didn't ask any questions and I think she hoped the distance would extend to mine and her daughter's relationship. It didn't.

"Can I stay at your place?" Elsie asks with a glance at my phone.

"Yeah, sure. I got something I gotta do at 8 though. Milo you wanna stay over too?" I look at him in the rear view mirror and give him a small smile.

"Yeah, I'll tell El's mom she is staying with me and tell my mom I'm stayin' with you." He nods as he starts texting the usual bullshit to their wardens.

I'm not stupid enough to think they haven't caught on to the lies judging by how often these two stay at my place but since Elsie's mom is still adjusting to single life and Milo's parents have become very hands off over the years no one has called us out. I pay and thank Kelley at the window, she is still cute but I am beyond hook ups now. I am hung up on the girl in my front seat and everyone seems to know it but her. Which is a good thing because she deserves someone so much better than me. She deserves a Milo. He could give her anything she wanted. Least that's what you tell yourself. Unfortunately, she hasn't shown much romantic interest in either of us other than a few stolen moments over the literal decade we've been friends.

The first time someone tried to tell her that her two best friends were hopelessly in love with her, she'd laughed at them. Listing off all the potential and great qualities we held and how there was absolutely no way either of us would want to settle down with her. As it became more of a common occurrence she had started getting angry and defensive, saying it was messed up they'd try to split us up like that. After that, we had started telling people not to mention it or I should say threatening people to leave it the hell alone in my case. I don't understand why she is so against being with Milo. Or me. Not that I'd let anything really happen between us, she is way too smart to be held down by me. Right? Then again, she does keep running back to Jett so maybe she is just really into the bad-boy thing.

I rest my hand on her thigh as we drive and pretend she really is my girl. It is a fantasy I play in my head often and hell the more I think about it the more I want it to be real. Swallowing hard as I pull up to my complex I make an impulse decision.

"Go on up Milo, I wanna talk to Elsie for a minute." He meets my gaze for a second and shrugs, completely oblivious to the knife I am about to stab in his back. We'd agreed way back in first grade that I wouldn't date El, that I wouldn't even try. But we aren't kids anymore and I don't want to play second string anymore.

I want Elsie to be my girl for real and finally stop her from running back to that jerk off Jett.

Milo leaves with the food and a little pang of guilt hits me in the chest knowing I could very well lose both of my friends in the next 5 minutes.

"Elsie, why won't you date me or Milo? Or me AND Milo for fucks sake?" I don't even breathe as I watch her expressions carefully. First there is shock, then anger and finally an adorable deep blush as she mauls her bottom lip. I reach out with my thumb and gently save it from her nervous attack.

"Mason… I don't want to be with Milo." She finally states.

"And me?" I press.

"I … I love you. I'd … I think I'd marry you but I know Milo has some pretty intense feelings for me and I don't want to hurt him." She sags like a weight has been lifted with her confession. My heart fucking soars and crash lands with her words.

"I love you too." I admit with a grin. In my mind, this was it. I love her and she loves me and Milo can man up and get over it. That is until I realize she isn't meeting my gaze. After several moments of hoping she'd just fucking look at me, I start to get angry. Of course it can't ever be that easy with El. "You're telling me that we love each other but you won't be with me because another man wants you and you don't want to fucking hurt him?"

"I don't want anything to change…" She insists but she still won't meet my eyes. I'm not gentle like Milo when I grip her chin and force her to look at me with a possessiveness I rarely let her see.

"It already has. You're mine now and I'm telling Milo to back off. I've waited for this moment way too long, I've tried all these years to convince you to date Milo. To like him more than me because I know I'm not what you deserve but now I know we feel the same. I am not letting you slip away."

"Don't you dare!" She snaps, trying to jerk away from my grasp. "Mason, not now. After graduation, please just not now." She switches back to begging and damn me it works.

"Kiss me and I'll let it wait until graduation." I counter with a smirk. She rolls her eyes but smiles. Leaning over she places the lightest kiss on my lips and I let her. I won't force her for more but that kiss will be my oxygen until she graduates.

Chapter 4

Mason
8 years later - Present day

"Rhett! Get out here!" Milo calls me from the main car bay. No one calls him Milo anymore though, and no one calls me Mason. Nope, we are in witness protection and have been for the last 7 years. We were relocated half a dozen times before things finally seemed to cool and we decided to open up the shop together. I fix the cars and Milo, or Liam as he is known now, fixes the books to cover the money we've been laundering for the Celio family here in Houston. It's probably how we've managed to stay put so long and it's the Celio contacts that are finally tracking down our girl.

"What?" I ask as I near him wiping my hands off on an oil rag. He is wearing a crisp white button down and slacks, he says he needs to look professional for his role. I, however, am very content in my wifebeater tank tops and oily jeans.

"That car look familiar to you?" He points directly out to the car waiting to be pulled into the bay and I could've kissed the man.

"My fucking camaro!" I jump like a kid on crack and race over to it, yanking the door and thankfully finding it unlocked. Leaning in, I immediately reach for the passenger seat. Yup, Elsie's name is still there. Resting my head on the center console I take a minute to compose myself feeling like I am the closest I have been to her in seven long damn years and it has me on the edge of weeping. Pulling myself out of the car I look to Liam with hope and tears in my eyes. He knows my next question and he slowly nods before breaking down into tears right there himself.

I drop to my knees on the concrete beside my car, hanging into the open door for support and sob. Thanking a God I don't believe in that we'd finally had a breakthrough. After a few minutes of balling our eyes out together on the floor like a couple of pansies I clear my throat and stand not bothering to wipe my face.

"Where is she? When can we see her?" I stare at him with all the gratitude in the damn world for keeping us together and never giving up even when I had no more fight to give.

"Hospital over on highway 3, Ralph called me 'bout five minutes ago and then Juan dropped the car off." He doesn't look happy though, relieved yes but not happy. Why isn't he happy? We have our girl back! Right?

"Let's go! Close shop! Whats the fucking hold up man?!" I am bouncing on the balls of my feet ready to say fuck the shop completely and haul ass.

"She hasn't woken up yet." He says solemnly. I stare at this man that I'd been through hell with and I've never felt more alone than when his words land like a lead brick in my stomach.

"What do you mean?" I ask slowly, cautious not to break my own heart.

"I mean she is unconscious and has been since they found her. She is in bad shape, Rhett. Real bad. I'm going to go close up while you take a minute." He spins on his heel and leaves me there to spiral for a minute.

For some reason I have tried to convince myself that her kidnapping had been an accident and she was just lost all these years. A month before graduation she hadn't been feeling well and I'd let her lay down in the back of my car while Milo and I ran into the store to pick up some stuff. We'd gotten a little carried away and taken longer than we had initially meant to. When we got back to the parking lot we both saw a man who I once knew as Bullet murder Jett Starkal in broad daylight. Then he'd jumped in my still running camaro and stole away the love of my life.

After calling the police, we'd learned that Bullet wasn't some small-time dealer. No, I'd been working for a crime family's tradesmen. I'd thought it was all drugs but it wasn't - they mostly dealt in flesh apparently. I'd vomited when I learned exactly what horrible things I had been helping happen.

Sliding into my old car I lean my head on the steering wheel that is still slightly misshapen from the many tantrums I'd had as a teenager and practiced breathing like Liam had taught me the day she had been taken and has practiced with me every day since. I had been young and foolish to associate with the people I had, but Liam never lets me wallow for too long. Forcing me to get my GED and do a technical course while we were on the East coast so that I'd have a trade skill. A legit way to make money. He'd done college online, he did accounting for a while before we opened the shop and paid for my record to be wiped clean. I don't know what I would've done without him. The back passenger door opens and I jump spinning around to find Liam smiling at me sheepishly with a shrug.

"Feels wrong to sit in her seat." He says gently rubbing the fabric of the back seat.

"Feels weird to have you in my back seat again..." I stare at him for what feels like a long time and try to see the annoying, golden boy I'd painted him to be in my mind all those years ago but nowhere on the sleek, hardened man in front of me do I recognize the Milo I'd grown up with. The familiar painful throb of loss rolls through my body and I turn my gaze to watch where I am heading as I start the car and begin to pull out to distract myself from the tidal waves of emotion threatening to drown me right now. "Buckle up."

"Never thought you'd have become a stickler for the rules." He chuckles but I hear the calming click of the belt latching into place.

"Yeah, well, guess I found out I wasn't hot shit after all." I joke back but it is half-hearted because both statements are true. "Where did they find her?"

"In a storage container with your car and a couple of kids. Barely got there in time to stop it from leaving the port." He sounds detached but I know him better than that. He must be on a similar rollercoaster of emotions as I am about this. "They found her tied up naked, said she is pretty battered. A camera was streaming her just laying there. The cops think someone is going to be very pissed when they don't get their shipment but Ralph said they'd take care of it."

I remain silent as I think over his words trying to prepare myself for what she might look like. Would she want to move in with us when she woke up? Would she even be her anymore? I can't even begin to imagine the hell she might've been through in the last seven years. Seven goddamn years stolen from her, from us. She didn't even graduate high school. She never saw the delayed acceptance letter from Harvard.

Her mom hadn't been able to handle losing her daughter and shot herself two weeks later. Her dad had overdosed on some pills not long after burying his ex-wife. How would we break the news that they are gone? Or that Milo's family had given him an ultimatum that day she was taken, and he'd chosen me?

Liam is all I have in this world and now we'll get a shot at happiness with Elsie again. No way am I cutting him out this time. Over the years we had talked about the what-ifs and whens, coming to the agreement that we'd share her. Care for her and support her in any way she would let us when she finally came home to us. She'd be able to set the boundaries and pace and we'd fall in line without complaint to just have our trio complete again. He hadn't even been mad at me when I told him about the day she confessed she loved me, and how I had practically forced her to agree to toss his feelings aside for me.

I pull into the main lot for the hospital and stare up at the building that now houses Elsie's sweet face somewhere within its walls. I feel Liam's hand rest on my shoulder and shudder.

"Let's go see our girl." He encourages before stepping out of the car. I am a step behind him the whole way to the front desk. This is how things are now. Liam leads, speaks and makes decisions while I follow him around like the ghost of a man haunting his anchor.

"Hello, I'm looking to visit a patient that was recently brought in." He explains with a tight smile for the receptionist. She is pretty, honey colored from her hair to her perfectly manicured nails. I wonder if Elsie would want to get her nails done some time. "Elsie Parker is her legal name but… with the circumstance I don't know if they'd use a different name." He trails off waiting while she tip-taps on the keyboard.

"Room 884." She supplies with a sad smile and gestures to the elevators behind her. I follow Liam and can't stop the tears leaking from my eyes. We are about to see our girl after so long of looking and running and hoping - it feels surreal. Liam wipes my cheeks and gives me a watery smile while we wait for the elevator.

"Can't let her know you've turned into a big softy straight away." He jokes as we enter the elevator and start the ascent to the 8th floor. I huff out a choked laugh for his benefit and try to pull myself together.

We exit on to the floor and something in both of

us shifts. The air around us seems to almost vibrate. We stand straighter, our strides holding a purpose they haven't before. In sync, we search the floor for the right room but when we are faced with those three little numbers neither of us move to open the door.

"Mason…" Milo whispers.

"Yeah, Milo?" I whisper back.

"I'm scared." He breathes.

"Me too." Then I grasp his hand and pull us both into the room just like on the first day of kindergarten.

Chapter 5

Mason
3 years prior

I sit on the floor of the apartment I share with Milo, or fucking Liam I guess, and carefully cradle the old shoe box. 'Remember Me' is scrawled on top in messy handwriting and purple crayon. I lean in and kiss the little thumb print heart she had added when we were in fifth grade. Running my hands carefully over the hot pink rhinestones that make a crooked border for her treasure box I blink back tears not wanting to taint this piece of her. The cardboard still smells slightly of the perfume I'd stolen for her in middle school. She hadn't known it was stolen and wore it all the time.

I swallow, setting it down on the hard floor like it is a bomb that might go off and take another swig out of the bourbon bottle I'd been nursing since Milo passed out on the floor next to me. He is absolutely wasted and needs sleep so I try to stay quiet as I guide the lid off the box and inhale deeply. Remember me. "How could we ever forget?" I answer the disembodied voice in my head outloud like the drunkard I am. "The most beautiful voice in the whole wide world." I murmur as I begin slowly pulling out her most prized possessions.

She told me once that the only things in her remember me box were the things she felt she could never part with. It was her if-the-house-was-burning-down catch all plan. It was the answer to every stupid what-if question about being stranded on an island or some bullshit. It held everything she said she wouldn't be herself without. The space that held the broken pieces of my heart felt like it was reliving the shattering all over again as I wondered who she was today, having gone so long without these pieces of herself. Without us. In one little shoe box, she had claimed to contain all the things that completed her.

It is mostly things Milo and I had given her. Even the horrible drawings we'd made in elementary school and the first pencil she had 'borrowed' from me. It held in its depths lockets and love notes between best friends and old photos from cheap print booths. I never understood her obsession with hoarding this stuff, but man I am glad she did because once a year on her birthday we get plastered and I look through her box and try to recall everything I ever knew about my peach.

Her lips were the color of a sweet, ripe peach so I'd showered her with all things peach scented and flavored. I close my eyes and try to remember what it had felt like when she had gifted me that single kiss as teenagers. Squeezing my eyes tighter, a sob wracked my body. DAMNIT! I can't remember what her lips had felt like.

I slowly put her things away and lay my head on Milo's chest as I sob. I am forgetting things about her and there is nothing I can do about it. A hollow chasm living where my organs should have been starts to fill with a broken agony I have been silently avoiding letting drown me since the day she had been taken. Tonight I don't fight the waves of grief as they crashed over me till my stomach rebels against the alcohol being shaken inside me. I turn just in time to vomit on the floor next to us and then lay back down. Defeated, exhausted and horrified we might never find her. It'll be all my fault. Wherever she is and whatever she is living through right now is on my shoulders.

"I'm so sorry I'm so sorry…" I mumble the mantra over and over until finally sleep takes pity on me and lets me slip away from my misery for a little while.

The headache comes into my reality first, closely followed by nausea and the sensation of twirling uncontrollably. Ugh…This is both the part I relish and dread of our yearly routine - the total anni-hilation of any water left in my body after near alcohol poisoning and sobbing my eyes out means the hangover can count towards my redemption. At least that's what I tell myself every year. Against my better judgment, I crack open an eyeball and wince as the light stabs an ice pick into my brain.

Leaning into the pain I open the other eye, the light streaming in from the sliding glass door tells me it is probably midday. Milo got up at some point and put a bottle of water and some pills by my face. Groaning, I push myself up into a seated position and guzzle them down. He must have cleaned up my vomit from last night too. Actually the apartment is suspiciously clean, having been mopped recently enough I can still smell the mild soap of Milo's preference. No trash or liquor bottles surround me.

"That was the last time. We can't keep destroying ourselves. It doesn't help her and it sure as hell doesn't help us." Milo announces from the threshold of the bathroom where he is holding the cleaning caddy in gloved hands. Ah, yes the other half of my redemption today. Every year is the 'last time' speech. "Don't look at me like that! I mean it, this is not happening again." He glowers at my bloodshot gaze for a long moment before hanging his head. "Just…take a shower." He walks past me with the weight of our lives on his shoulders clear as day. Each year I am reminded how much I fucked up and how the two people who always stuck by me are paying the most.

Standing up, I stumble to the bathroom and strip down, not bothering to shut the door. At this point we could be mistaken for a young gay couple, living in a small studio apartment together and sharing a bed means there really isn't any room for secrecy between the two of us and we like it that way. Or at least I like it that way. The shower is cold and I don't bother adjusting the water, letting the chill wake me from the fog clinging to me from last night.

"Please, please don't do this." I beg as my tears mix with the snot running down my face. Milo stands rigidly between me and his parents, facing them down.

"You can see what associating with him earned Els-" His mother begins to reason, trying to convince him to cut off all contact with me by going to a different location with the witness protection program.

"You don't get to say her name."Milo growls through clenched teeth. My heart is in my throat as I wait for him to do what he has always done and submit to his parents will.

"Enough." His dad snaps. "You go with him and you will never be welcomed back into our home." Milo rocks on his heel as the blow lands right where it was meant to. Me or them. How could they do that right now? When

our worlds are being ripped apart?! He recovers quickly and steps backwards until my hands find his arm and I cling to him for dear life. He seems to grow several inches as he straightens his back and levels to meet his father's gaze.

"Then go home and forget about me. Mason is my family and we will find her and we will be just fine without you." I shake uncontrollably and crumple into him with relief. His mother's shocked expression fills with hurt as his dad simply nods and begins to guide her away. He holds it together until they were out of sight and then we sink to the floor grasping onto each other. Another part of him died in that moment and I silently swore to help restore that light someday, somehow.

"Come on, you have to use soap." Milo's appearance means I have been standing in the freezing water far longer than I realized and I blink at him, noting that I hadn't pulled the shower curtain closed either. I nod and he stocks away as I close the curtain finally warming the water and getting washed up.

Somehow.

Chapter 6

Mason
Present Day

Time doesn't exist on the other side of her door. Still holding Liam's hand, I take in the large room. It has pale pink walls, an orange-tan couch under the windows that lines the far wall and two matching chairs that house police officers. The officer closest to us stands, he is a man we know all too well after all these years. Officer Hansley had been the responding officer to our frantic call when she was first taken, and he has been our handler ever since. Gray is invading his dark hair and stress has aged him far more than seven years should've. Just another person's life I need to atone for ruining in some way.

"Where is she?" I croak around the lump in my throat. Dear god, are we too late? Has something happened? My breathing speeds up as I take in the room. There isn't a bed, just some monitors framing where the bed containing the most important person in my life should have been.

"They took her down for an MRI. I'm glad you boys came when you did. She… I wanted to prepare you two a little bit." Hansley says as he shakes our hands. Tamping down my panic, I look to Liam who nods in understanding.

"They said she was pretty roughed up…" Liam trails off waiting for Hansley to fill in the blanks.

"Not as bad off as we initially thought. She's been drugged, that's why she isn't fully lucid yet so be prepared that she likely won't know who you are at all. She isn't here with us in our current reality when she is awake. She has been sleeping mostly and likely that'll continue while the drugs work their way out of her system." He gestures to the couch before sitting back down in his chair. I follow Liam and grip his hand tighter as we sit together. "Look, I know you boys want to take care of her but I'm not sure you're ready to take her on with the kind of care she will need."

"We are willing to get her any additional support she needs but she is coming home with us." Liam states matter-of-factly as he meets Hansley's gaze head on. I straighten and do my part as back up for his claim. Appearances are vital, Liam preaches that shit to me every chance he gets.

"She will have to agree to that." The other Officer chimes in with a clipped tone while taking us in head to toe and his expression clearly says he doesn't think we are the best option for her.

"She will." Liam supplies with a confidence I can't muster. It is my fault she got taken in the first place, I won't be surprised if she hates me.

"We can sort that out later. You boys know I only want what's best for all three of you." Hansley is clearly placating us but Liam doesn't take the bait.

"Sure. Now, what do we need to know before they bring her back in here?" He presses, guiding the conversation back to the matter at hand.

"She is real small. She's got some obvious bruising, her wrists and ankles look like they've been compressed for a long time, boys. We're talking years here. And she has rope burns all over her, poor thing. Scans showed they must've broken every bone in her body over the time she's been held captive but nothing is broken right now. They had her prepped for sale we think so her current condition physically isn't too bad. But the mental scars are likely deep and won't heal anywhere near as quickly as her body." Liam nods along with him and relaxes a bit so I relax too. Gesturing to the other cop, Hansley continued. "This is her handler, Officer Belton. He will be in charge of making sure she ends up where she will be happiest to start recovering, seeing to it that she gets all the care she needs and will intervene if ever there's another problem." My gaze slides to Belton's locked jaw and hard expression as he crosses his arms over his chest. He has dark, buzzed hair and a square jaw. The force has kept him in shape and I'm sure a lot of women find him attractive. "He is the one who found her and so far she has responded well to him." Of course she fucking has. I grind my teeth together and barely resist the urge to roll my eyes as jealousy surges through me.

"Thank you." Liam offers Belton sincerely. "We have the same goal and we will

"Theo." Belton offers in return with a slight nod. "We are going to be working together for a while. Might as well be on a first name basis. I'm not trying to take her away from you two, I just want what will be best for her recovery." The door to her room opens then and I inhale a deep breath watching the orderly roll her bed into place. Her hair is knotted and dirty as it halos around her in its rose gold glory, disappearing under her gown clad shoulders. Blankets cover her from just below her shoulders down, so only the bruise on the side of her neck that covers her ear and part of one cheek is visible. The orderly finishes hooking back up all the machines without a word and leaves the room in a hurry.

Liam tugs me along beside him as he approaches the bed. Elsie doesn't seem to have aged at all in my eyes. He guides me to sit on the edge of the bed and I reach out to place my hand over where hers is, leaving the blanket between us while he rounds the bed and does the same on the other side. I hear Hansley sniffle before clearing his throat and making shuffling sounds.

"I've got to get some air. I'll be back later on. Belton give me a call when she wakes up again or if you need anything." He announces before departing. Neither Liam nor I give any indication we heard him.

"Sure thing." Belton says in that deep voice of his that is likely going to color my every insecurity about her still wanting us for the foreseeable future. We stayed like that for hours, no one talking or moving. I barely blinked, hating the idea that I might miss the moment her beautiful eyes would open. Eventually, Belton went to grab dinner and Liam stood to stretch.

"Let's move the chairs closer so we can sit more comfortably. Probably still a while before she wakes up." He suggests quietly as he begins rearranging things. We'll be here until either she is discharged or tells us to kick rocks but I can't bring myself to move. I know Liam is right about us needing to take our comfort into account while we wait but moving away from her feels impossible as I continue to categorize her features again. Liam presses a chair facing her as close to the bed as possible and pulls on my arm. I fumble off the bed, not looking behind me as I follow his silent order while refusing to move my hand or my gaze from her.

"Do you think she will remember who we are?" I ask him in a small voice just as he rounds the bed to take a seat on the opposite side.

"I don't know, man. I hope so." He sounds exhausted and I almost suggest he should sleep but he continues talking. "You heard Hansley, she is still coming off whatever cocktail of black-market drugs they've had her on so I'm not holding my breath but I really hope she knows who we are. It'd suck if our first memory of her awake after all these years is her screaming in terror. That's probably more likely than the lovestruck reunion version I've been playing in my head though."

"Yeah." I nod and we fall back into a comfortable silence. Nurses flitted in and out of the room periodically and Theo brought us burgers which we ate like robots and after a while he stopped trying to make conversation, opting to lay on the couch for a nap when he received barely there replies. I never took my eyes off Elsie, counting her eyelashes and then her freckles forcing myself to start over whenever I lost count to keep my mind busy. Once I could hear Liam's breathing even out and deepening, indicating he too had nodded off, I reached out to touch her face but stopped just before making contact. Touching her skin would confirm that this was real and I want it to be real so badly but I'm terrified at the same time. There was no set plan for what to do after we found her because we never knew what condition she would be in - if she was even alive. But now, looking down at her, thinking about all the things that will change with her coming back into our lives seems never ending. She'd need to see doctors and therapists pretty regularly most likely and we'd need to buy her a bed. Liam and I have been sharing a queen-sized bed since we entered the witness protection program, would he want that to change now?

Taking a slow breath, I ever so gently brush my fingers over her temple. Cool, smooth, buttery soft skin meets my fingers and silent tears begin to roll down my cheeks. No matter what damage they've inflicted upon her, nothing about Elsie will ever be anything but soft. I continued to pet her slowly as I let reality sink in. She'd need clothes and some hygiene products for sure. I could build her a little reading area in the shop so she can always be close by. She leans into my hand a bit in her sleep and it soothes something in my soul, small pieces of my shattered heart finding their homes again.

I study her face intently from this new angle hunting for signs of what her story over the last seven years had entailed but not much has really changed in the years since I'd last seen her. Aside from the obvious bruise that is. And she is a little thinner than I remember but not to the point of looking like one of those girls with an eating disorder or anything. Her skin had always been pale, but maybe it was a little more gray than pink now. It's hard to tell since her hair and lips have always held an orangey tone which brings out all her pink hues as well. Her lashes flutter a little and my heart leaps into my throat. I freeze, hand hovering by her temple as I wait to see if she will open those big green eyes for me. After several minutes, I returned to petting her and let the tension leak from my body. She isn't waking up just yet.

Chapter 7

Liam
Present Day

Opening my eyes, I crack my neck as the room filters back in. Rhett is leaned over with his head resting on Elsie's bed. His light snoring signaling he finally fell asleep at some point and while I know his back is going to be hurting later I'm glad he is getting some rest. I lock eyes with Officer Theo Belton across Rhett's sleeping form where he is sitting up on the couch behind him.

"He's been asleep for at least an hour." He informs me in a low tone with a nod towards my best friend.

"Good. He needs it." I reply with a sigh while I get up to stretch my stiff body. Sleeping upright really doesn't bode well for good rest but it'll have to do. My body is a symphony of cracks and pops as I alleviate some of the stiffness. Glancing over, Theo is staring holes into me and I groan internally. It's stressful enough always having Rhett looking at me for direction or answers without adding an overbearing cop to the mix. "You have questions."

"I do. You want coffee before or after I ask them?" He is trying to soften the blow, which helps a little bit to take the edge off my nerves. I let him sit in silence for a moment though as I get comfortable again in my chair as a memory steals my attention.

"Ewwww!" Elsie covers her nose dramatically as she gets in Mason's Camaro. "Why do you insist on drinking coffee before exams?!" She glares at the offending cup in my hand.

"You know most people love the smell of coffee, right?" I need the caffeine to help recover from all the cramming I had to do last night. She is adorable when she is mad though and I can't hide my smile.

"If I was most people, you wouldn't like hanging out with me." She drops her hand with a grin that makes my heart thump faster.

"Look what I got done, babe." Mason rubs the headrest on the passenger seat she is sitting in. Turning around, she gasps and her eyes light up. She doesn't say anything as she traces the sparkly scrolled embroidery that wasn't there yesterday. "Now everyone will know that it is your seat forever."

"Oh my god...Thank you! I love it!" She squeals excitedly, doing little claps and bouncing in her seat.

"She hated the smell of coffee before, maybe you could grab us some Red Bulls or something in a bit?" I give him a halfhearted smile and lean back preparing myself for his interrogation.

"Sure thing. Hansley filled me in on the basics but what I want to know isn't in that case file. Who are you to each other?" In the case file, it labels us all as friends. I almost want to give him the same vague description, but he is going to be around for a while so I might as well help him understand the shit storm he strolled into.

"We were best friends. Lived next door to each other and met on the first day of kindergarten. Been family ever since." I sigh and Elsie sighs too in her sleep pulling an affectionate smile on to my face. "Everyone thought it'd be me and her getting married someday. Except for her anyway," I chuckle with Theo for a minute gazing at the stubborn girl who stole my heart a lifetime ago. "Nope she swore up and down there would never be anything more than friendship between any of us. Came out after she was taken that she and Rhett had confessed their feelings for each other and were planning to make it official after graduation. She never made it to graduation day." My tone has gone stony and I can feel the scowl forming deeper wrinkles into my skin. "That's 'bout all there is to know I guess." I tilt my head to stare at Theo who looks like he may have swallowed his tongue for a minute.

"Bullshit. There has to be a lot more to the story

than that. You don't go through what you all have for a simple crush, even a close childhood friendship doesn't usually warrant this level of commitment."

"Family sticks together." I explain blandly and go back to looking at Elsie and Rhett, a clear dismissal from this conversation as the familiar weight of those words settles onto my shoulders. Maybe I'm not ready to be that helpful after all. Taking it on the chin, he mutters something about getting food and leaves again. I'm certain that he has another hundred questions swirling around in his head and I can't blame the guy. He pulled this poor, beautiful angel out of a storage container just a few hours ago and now has two rough around the edges looking guys claiming to be the best option for her. Two guys that have been pretty tight lipped as well. I get it, I do. We're coming off as cagey, too rough and possibly even unstable but until she opens her eyes this is all anyone is getting.

Trying to explain how we orbit around her and have been absolutely fucking lost since she was taken is just too much right now. As it is, I have to make sure Rhett continues to function while we wait. Make sure he eats, drinks, gets up to take a piss every now and then. I was even tempted to blow some air in his face earlier so he'd blink. He has been carrying around this guilt and drowning in self-loathing for so long I'm not sure he knows what it would feel like to not have those things anymore.

Elsie looks worn down and broken. Her usually glowing complexion is ashen and gray. She has one large bruise like she was slammed into a countertop or something along with a smattering of other smaller bruises that are in a range of stages of healing. Someone must have hacked at her hair at some point because it's noticeably choppy even though it's a tangled, dirty mess around her right now. Her right ear is pierced now, though there is nothing in the tiny hole. I wonder why they pierced her ear and only the one. Was she tagged like cattle? My stomach churns making me momentarily regret the burger from earlier. A soft knock at the door saves me from those thoughts as a pretty nurse in lavender scrubs comes in.

"Hey, sorry. I just need to get her vitals again." I scoot my chair out of her way so she can get to Elsie easier. "I'm Rebekah by the way, I'll be taking care of her tonight. If there is anything you need just let me know." Her chocolate colored hair is twisted up into a messy bun with a thick headband to hold it out of her way as she works. She is cute in a conventional way, all long lean legs and subtle curves. If my life hadn't taken such a tragic turn, I might have even considered asking for her phone number but alas her worlds and mine are likely galaxies apart.

"Thanks, I'm Liam and that's Rhett. Do you

happen to know if it is likely she might wake up tonight?"

"Oh heavens, no. She is so medicated I'm sure she won't wake up again until the doctors are good and ready with a better plan." She rolls her eyes over her shoulder to show me how unimpressed she is with them. "First time she woke up, she apparently gave everyone within a southern minute a heart attack. Poor thing was screaming and hollering like her life depended on it according to the intake nurse. The second time? Well, let's just be thankful Officer yum-tum was here to play hero while they got her sedated." Her drawl is thicker now than when she'd first introduced herself and something about her flippant attitude makes me twitchy.

"Ah. Alright." I watch as she finishes checking over the IV bag before giving me a little finger wave and ducking out to see her next patient no doubt. Rhett sits up with a groan and scrubs his hand down his face but I'm distracted by a quiet, frazzled exchange by the door and moments later Theo reappears.

"I've got three kinds of Red Bull, Italian subway sandwiches and Hansley let it slip y'all are partial to honey buns so I got some of those, too." Theo announces as he starts unloading onto a small rolling table. Once his hands are free he places them on his hips and stares straight at Rhett. "Now, I've got questions and I need y'all to answer them so we can all be on the same page; since we are all on the same team it only seems fair to me."

Grand, just grand.

Chapter 8

Liam
Present Day

Scrunching up my nose as Theo hands Rhett a blueberry flavored Red Bull, I unwrap the sandwich partially because I'm hungry but also so I can use my chewing as a reason to stay quiet during this conversation. Clearly since I hadn't been as cooperative as he'd have liked earlier, Theo has decided to sweet-talk Rhett into being his source. *Good luck, this is going to be a good show.* I manage to stifle my chuckle with my sub, leaning back in my chair.

"So, Rhett, tell me more about your girl here?" Theo prompts casually as he gets himself situated on the couch.

"Why?" Rhett has turned so his back is facing the officer. Whether that is to help him ignore the questioning or just so he can return to drilling burr holes into Elsie's head with his eyes though I can't tell.

"Well, like I said, we are all on the same team and I'm just trying to get to know my team better."

"Why?" Rhett repeats in a bored tone as he sips his drink.

"It's important for everyone on a team to know all the details so we can work together…" Theo drags out his explanation slowly, like it might be setting in that Rhett plans to be less help than a petulant child. "Touchy subject, I get it. Why don't you tell me more about you then?"

"Why?" Rhett smirks at me and I stuff my sand-wich in my mouth to try and muffle my laughter. I almost feel bad for the guy. *Almost.*

"Why not?" Theo counters. I slow my chewing as my eyes ping pong between the two of them and the silence stretches uncomfortably long. Rhett is lightly petting El's hand for a minute before abruptly chugging the rest of his drink and tossing it in the trash can across the room Kobe style. It sinks with a clatter.

"Ko-bee!" Me and Rhett call in unison.

"Kobe!" Theo echoes with less enthusiasm, both of us give him a look of disgust before returning to ignoring him. "Come on guys, give me an inch here - "

"I did give you an inch." I remind him calmly.

"Okay, that's fair. But I need something more to

go on here if you want my vote in letting her go home with you two because right now I doubt y'all have any ability to help her. You've been rude, surly and far too quiet to be considered normal since you got here." He grabs the back of his neck and sighs heavily. "You haven't had the easiest hand in life and I'm sure that has made you both weary of people, especially cops but I really am just trying to help here."

Rhett meets my gaze and a silent conversation seems to pass between us. He wants to know if I think we should give him more of an insight into our lives or not. *Of course, he is looking to you for the final decision.* There is nothing more humbling or honoring than knowing Rhett trusts me like that. Setting my sandwich down, I stand and stretch.

"Let's take a walk." I gesture with a nod to Theo and he joins me as we exit the room; our strides in sync. Stepping into the too quiet, sterile hall I head to where I see Rebekah at the nurses station.

"Oh! Yes, is there something I can help you with?" She flutters her lashes and gives me a sweet smile.

"We are just going to step out for a bit, could you give Officer Belton here a call if she wakes up? I know you said it wasn't likely but…" I give her my best boy-next-door smile and she visibly melts a little.

"Yes, yes. Of course, honey!" With a gracious

nod, I turn to lead Theo to the elevators. He gives a murmured thanks as well and follows obediently. I guess I have gotten pretty good at leading over the last few years. I used to wonder how coaches and favored teachers got people to listen to them so easily, having asked them regularly I finally understand how they didn't really know the answer either.

The ride to the bottom floor is quiet and surprisingly we aren't stopped on the way down for other passengers to board. It is getting late so I guess most visitors have gone home for the night. Theo stands with trained confidence and the air of patience only decent police officers master. Even Hansley became fairly heated the first couple of times he had to deal with any push back from us. *Ding.* Stepping out of the elevator I purposely avoid acknowledging the receptionist and lead him to the parking lot, the humid night air a welcome change from the static cold of the hospital. Reaching Rhett's Camaro, I lean on the hood with my arms crossed to face him.

"Everything I told you earlier is the truth. What exactly would make you feel more like backing us up when we go to take her home?" I keep my tone even, my face neutral and try to get a read on if his response will be a lie or not.

"What can you offer her?" He crosses his arms and stares me down.

"Shelter, food, water, moral support, a deep under-standing of who she was and acceptance of whoever she has become." I refuse to break eye contact.

"Nearly anyone could do those things for her, a lot of them probably a lot better than you. I looked into your life. You own a garage that isn't doing so great this year, if it wasn't for your *investors* I'm not sure you'd still be open. Only one apartment is leased between the two of you, and it's a one bedroom. Barely eight hundred square feet of space for two bachelors who spend all their time at work probably isn't so bad, but add in a third person? A person who might want some privacy and things might not be so peachy. Did you think of that? What if she has panic attacks or can't handle loud noises? You ever dealt with those things?" His line of questioning should have pissed me off, but instead I decide to answer what he is really asking. *How do I know she will be more than okay with you?*

"We've been saving for years in case this day ever came. We have plenty of money to get a bigger apartment if she wants that but I doubt she will. Mason - back before he was Rhett, before her kidnapping - used to have panic attacks. His dad murdered his mom at the end of kindergarten. After she was taken, it got bad again so I have plenty of experience caring for someone overrun with grief. Navigating her triggers might be a bit trickier but I swear if I can't help her I will find someone who can. If you've looked that closely then you already know that besides our choice of investors, we have both been squeaky clean since she was kidnapped." I take a deep breath as I watch some of the tension ease from his body. "Look, I'm not going to lie and say we have it all figured out because we don't. There was no way for us to really plan - for a while we didn't even know if she was alive."

"Okay. So tell me about how differently you two will behave with her than you do with other people? So far, you've been pretty civilized but your buddy is ticking time bomb." He nods and comes to stand beside me, leaning on the car as well now.

"Rhett is already treating her like a porcelain doll. You can expect him to probably be too much, at least at first. He is going to baby her for as long as she will let him." I smile just thinking about it.

"And you?" He prompts.

"I plan to hang back a bit. Give her some space and try to figure out exactly what kind of support she needs during each stage of her recovery, you know?"

"Yeah, it's not a bad plan. I will be with you guys for a while. Depending on her, I may need to move in for a little bit but at the very least I will be making house visits often. You got an extra bed?"

"Nope."

"A couch?" He chuckles.

"Nope." I join him in laughing as he looks at me in disbelief.

"A…recliner?" He asks through his laughter.

"Better bring an air mattress." We both lose it and laugh until tears form in our eyes. It isn't really that funny but envisioning him trying to move into our small barren apartment is amusing. "Honestly, me and Rhett have been sharing a bed for years. I'm kind of hoping she will just want to be piggy in the middle." He scrubs a hand over his face as our laughter dies out. "Tell me about you then."

"My story is not nearly as interesting as yours. I grew up in the west suburbs of Houston with both my parents and my two brothers. I'm the middle child. My dad was on the force and then my brother joined up so it just felt right to do the same. I did some specialty training and met Hansley through that. No girlfriend, no pets. I share an apartment with my younger brother - he works for the fire department." Shrugging he seems indifferent to how blessedly normal his life has been. "Look, I know this is your life - a big chapter of it at least. But this is an assignment for me, a small blip. Maybe a success story I pass along down the road to a rookie. I want the best for her as much as I do the next person."

"I appreciate the honesty, Theo. Rhett probably isn't going to open up to you but he trusts I'll make sure you know what you need to. Don't take it personally, he is just that way." Theo nods and pulls out his phone as it begins to ring.

"Officer Belton." He greets them but I can't hear what the other person is saying. Just in case it is that nurse I start walking back inside, not bothering to wait for confirmation.

I breeze past reception and push the button for the elevator with Theo right on my heels. He continues to murmur into the phone quietly while we wait. Finally, a ding accompanies the elevator doors to my left popping open and I rush inside. Not waiting, I press the button for her floor and start pressing the one to close the doors faster. Theo shoots me a glare as he slides in beside me and hangs up his call.

"She woke up." He informs me.

"I figured." I'm tapping my thumb against my thigh but otherwise seem to be doing okay at keeping a lid on how angsty I feel. I shouldn't have left Rhett in there by himself. Not even for a minute. Her panic could set off his panic. What if he gets kicked out? Or if his first memory of her waking up becomes his new worst nightmare? I shouldn't have left.

The doors open and I make quick work of finding her room again. Rhett is sitting in the hallway, knees to chest with his arms wrapped around them. He isn't hysterically crying so that's a good sign.

I slow and let Theo pass by as he goes inside her room, surprised by how much I trust he will handle whatever is on the other side of the door while I attend to Rhett after our little conversation.

A team.

"What happened?" I ask as I slide down the wall to sit beside him.

"I was just sitting there and she started talking. Scared the shit out of me." He stares at me wide eyed like he has just seen a ghost.

"What'd she say?" I put an arm over his shoulders and scoot a little closer.

"She… she asked for some water." He half laughs, bewildered. "I jumped up to get some and told her to hang on just a second and it's like that's when she really woke up. Her eyes got real big and the monitor started blaring. A couple nurses came rushing in and kicked me out before either of us could do anything else." He shakes his head like he can't believe it actually happened.

"They called Theo so maybe they will let us back in soon and she will be awake, yeah?" I encourage him with a small squeeze.

"She sounds the same as before man, she even had the gravely edge she used to get in the mornings." He is beaming at me and my chest aches. I don't know the last time I've seen him this happy. His chin dimple is even showing and I can't help the watery smile growing on my face.

Chapter 9

Elsie
Present Day

This room is too cold. My hands shake as a woman in light purple scrubs fusses over me, asking me questions. I can't focus enough to know how to answer her so I just stare at where I saw Mason disappear. No, that can't be right because why would he be here? I swat at the icy hands of an older nurse who tries to pry the blanket away from me. Again she is speaking but it just sounds like buzzing. I can't breathe. I can't think. Did I see Mason? Am I dreaming? No, it's too cold to be a dream. Hallucinating maybe.

A man enters the room and I hold the blanket closer to me, earning myself a grumpy look from the older nurse who is speaking to the man now. He looks vaguely familiar, the uniform tells me he is a cop. Police and hospital staff means I've been rescued, right? The woman in the purple scrubs lightly touches my shoulder and I look over at her. Her mouth is moving but the words sound weird, like I'm under water.

"My…my ears!" Even my own voice sounds kind of far away and I search her face to see if I should be feeling panicked about this. Did they already know something was wrong with my ears? She leans in with an otoscope to check both ears before holding up both hands in front of her in a placating motion and then struts over to the white board where she writes in big letters.

"My … ear…drum…is…damaged?" I read it out loud and sag a little when she nods before she starts writing on the board again. "Is…is Mason h-here?" I ask while she is busy writing about when the doctor will be back to see me. She glances at the cop and again I can see they are talking but nothing makes sense to me. He gives me a thumbs up and I gasp, covering my mouth with both of my hands that are still under my blanket. "A-a-and…Milo?" I'm scared to ask, but I need to know. Again he gives me a thumbs up and I feel like I might be going into shock.

I feel like sobbing and leaping from the bed with joy at the same time but my limbs feel staticy and the world seems so far away. Why aren't they here? Where did he go? Did the nurse make him leave? How did they even know I was here - did my parents call them?

"My parents?" I ask, dropping my hands into my lap. Based on the jabbing pain in my ear, I'm pretty certain I asked that much louder than I'd meant to. The cop's face goes blank and he shakes his head no. I pause for a moment and then ask, "Not yet? Are they coming?" I think I did better with the volume that time. Instead of answering me, he starts talking to the nurse again who disappears out into what I guess is the hallway. I'm about to ask again thinking maybe he didn't hear me when Mason appears and I stop short.

He is all man now, taller than the cop and built like a linebacker. His hair is shorter than he used to keep it and he is wearing a blue tank top with dark smudges on it. His jeans don't fit quite right, they are a little too loose and are covered in all kinds of stains. But there is no doubt in my mind that this is Mason Pikes. I can feel the smile on my face and he doesn't wait to approach the bed.

Too soon, too fast he goes to wrap me in his arms and I can't help but to cower away from him. He freezes and says something but I furiously shake my head and point at the board and then my ear. Another familiar face hovers just behind Mason's shoulder now. Milo, looking like a full grown Ken doll with his gold blonde hair, chiseled features and tanned skin. He offers me a small smile and I almost don't notice when he begins physically guiding Mason backwards by the shoulders. I cringe waiting for Mason to snap, or push him off but he doesn't. He just accepts the chair that has been pushed behind him and reaches out slowly with his palm up.

I can handle this. I can do this. I shake as I reach my hand out to meet his and sigh as his warmth spreads over my skin. Milo has moved to the other side of me now and we repeat the interaction of slowly reaching to hold each other's hands. Warily, I glance at the officer standing at the foot of my bed having what appears to be a heated discussion with that older nurse.

He must feel my gaze on him because he stomps over to the board.

ARE YOU IN ANY PAIN?

"No… not really." I reply, hoping my volume is right this time. He gestures at me as he argues with the nurse again who looks exasperated.

DO YOU WANT TO GO BACK TO SLEEP?

"No! No, really I feel fine!" Judging by the worried exchange between Mason and Milo and the disapproving glare from the nurse I guess I don't seem very convincing. I really don't want to be trapped in my nightmares again though. It feels like it has been days of endless psychological torture in my own mind. The cop continues to go back and forth with the woman until the younger nurse comes back in. Popping a hip out, she addresses the older woman with the same air of a mother chiding a rebellious teenager.

Finally, the older nurse throws her hands up in the air and points at my guys, giving them some kind of stern warning before she leaves. Lavender nurse shoots me a wink before she skips out after ol' grumpy pants.

"My parents?" I ask again. The cop keeps a neutral expression but all eyes move to focus on Milo as he pulls out his cellphone, slowly typing out a response for me. Interesting, he was definitely not our usual spokesperson back then but it could be that he is the only one still speaking to our parents. That would make sense considering my mom was always looking for a reason to dislike Mason anyway. It's not his fault some guy decided to hijack his car but I am certain she has twisted the story to make him the villain somehow. Still, I've prayed silently for years to see her again. I've been caressed by death's sweet embrace and just before that chilling moment I had wished for just one more conversation with her to make it all better. Fill in the holes of our realities and find some common ground - maybe she'd hold me like she did before life got so complicated.

Mason's grip tightens on my hand and I look over to him, taking in how tired he looks. I'm sure I don't look any better but he used to seem so carefree, his leg is bouncing as he stares between me and Milo. Stress rolls off him in waves, my mom and his relationship must be really strained if he is this agitated already. I study the cop again while I wait. He looks so familiar…

My shoulders scream from being twisted behind me like this for so long. I shift a little trying to find relief but the rope binding me is intricately laced from my biceps to my wrists with no allowance for even the slightest adjustments. My ankles are also somehow bound into his rope work and are stuck just below the small of my back making it arch uncomfortably and my knees spread as my body tries not to rip itself apart from being held in this position. I'm laid on my stomach as usual so that my bindings can be clearly seen, at least that is the explanation Reaper gives every time he finishes securing yet another horrifyingly detailed binding. I'm pretty sure it's so my near permanent nudity can be exploited. He has never left me for this long though. I can't tell for sure how long it has been inside this new storage container but the heat during the day is far more tortuous than during the evening. By my guess it's been three days since he last visited.

Someone else has been coming and going, the shuffling of feet and whimpers tells me I'm not alone but my position makes talking hard and whoever else is here probably wouldn't reply anyway. Still the flashing from the red light on the video camera behind me reflects off the wall of the container and I know I'm being watched. I've been constantly watched for years now but time doesn't take the edge off the crawling feeling that lives on my skin.

The container door swings open loudly and my field of vision is flooded with light unexpectedly. There is yelling, lots of yelling and I wish I could move to look and see what is happening. I take a deep breath and close my eyes. Whatever it is, Reaper won't let anything worse happen to me.

I am His and he is greedy. I am His and he is greedy. I am His.

I repeat the sick, twisted mantra and try to ignore how calming it is to me now. I've repeated those words so many times that I am certain of their truth. I might get out of the trade someday, but I will always belong to Reaper and there is something akin to comfort in that knowledge. A soft touch to my face has me opening my eyes on an unfamiliar face. His dark blue uniform used to mean something to me - it used to mean safety and justice but I know now there are more dirty cops than there are criminals in this life. I shriek for Reaper but it's like I am under water. I can't hear myself. I can't breathe!

I jolt and blink rapidly as Milo taps his thumb on my hand gently, his face full of concern. My eyes are watery and I swallow hard trying to clear my head. That's the cop that found me. Milo shows me his phone again so I attempt to focus on what he has typed for me.

You are going to have a lot of questions and I promise to answer them. Your parents are not coming. They are dead, El. I am so sorry. But Mason and I are going to take care of you I promise.

Tears stream down my face, guilt and nausea tussle in my stomach partly because it seems surreal that I survived all *that* and somehow still don't get my reunion. I should feel overwhelmed with grief for my parents, but mostly because in this moment of safety, with my two best friends that I have longed for all this time I should be leaning into them. I should feel comforted somehow by the fact they are the ones to tell me my parents are dead. I don't though. I close my eyes and picture the man who has owned me for the last five years, longing for the comfort only he can give me.

I am His and he is greedy.

Chapter 10

Rhett
Present Day

She hasn't reopened her eyes again in the fifteen minutes since Liam dropped that fucking bomb shell on her. I get ripping the band-aid off with bad news but there had to have been a better way. The skin of her arms are just big bruises covered in rope burns at this point. Her pretty little hands are puffy, swollen and bruised in odd patterns. My stomach churns and I force the tears stinging the backs of my eyes to subside. She needs support right now. I have to keep my shit together.

"Did she go back to sleep?" Officer Fuck Head asks. Why the hell does he need to be here, anyway? She seemed scared of him so maybe it would be better if he left. Anxiety, guilt and jealousy are coursing through my veins making me feel jittery and angry. Taking a deep breath I remind myself he *has* to be here. It's his job.

"I don't think so. I think she is just processing. It

can't be easy to think all the bad things have stopped and then be hit with more bad news." Liam muses quietly. With her hearing problem she probably can't hear us but his words make me want to comfort her somehow. Scared to touch her bruises, I rub my thumb in quick succession on the hand I'm holding.

Slowly, she tilts her head towards me and opens her eyes. In her eyes I see a familiar pain and I wish I could hand her a bottle of something strong to numb her from the inside out. What had they done when my parents went off the rails…?

Milo's parents ushered all three of us into their spare bedroom as far away from the commotion still happening at my house as possible. His dad set up his movie projector and Elsie picked out something to watch while Milo went to the kitchen with his mom to get food. It's too early for a movie. It's still light outside.

"Mason…" Elsie whispers from beside me.

"Yeah?"

"When I'm sad, my mom sometimes bundles me up like a burrito and holds me. I'm not big enough to hold you yet but I could roll you into a burrito?" She offers. It's silly but I nod anyway. She jumps up and lays a blanket flat. "Okay now lay in the middle with your head off the blanket, yeah like that!" Smiling, she starts tucking the blanket in snuggly around me. It's not my blanket and it smells like Milo's mom but as she keeps tugging and tucking the comfort of being wrapped up

sets in and I take a big gulp of air. "There...now let's just roll you over there so you can see the movie." She huffs and puffs as she struggles to get me to roll and I can't help because of how tight she has me wrapped. I start to laugh first and then she starts giggling.

"What's happening?" Milo asks, his arms overflowing with the snacks we usually aren't allowed. We both start laughing harder because I'm a burrito and El is weak and Milo looks ridiculous carrying so much food! And then I start to cry because my mom is dead and my dad is gone and all I wanted was to spend my afternoon with my friends like any other day but now we are all laughing and crying. My dad killed my mom.

Milo sets the food down and they both manage to roll me to a better spot then they cover all three of us with a big heavy blanket and they squeeze in tight on either side of me. They've stopped laughing. I think we're all just crying.

"Are you hungry?" I ask too loudly, snapping out of my thoughts and she cringes away from me. Fuck, I should know better. Liam saves my plunder though by showing her a text relaying the same question.

"I feel like I might throw up." She admits quietly. Liam starts typing again and I stand up. I can't take just sitting here. I need to *do* something to help her feel better.

"I'll tell the nurse." I leave the room before anyone

reacts. Stepping out of her room feels wrong but so welcome at the same time. She looks so broken and it's my fault! I am the reason she is laying in that bed, why her parents are gone, why she ever had to see the evil side of the world. I don't deserve to be in there right now. Her room isn't far from the nurses station and several nurses glance up as I approach. "She feels sick." I announce to no one in particular. Just as a male nurse is about to start asking questions, her night nurse Rebekah pops up from the corner.

"I got it!" She chirps as she starts towards me and tilts her head as she scrutinizes my expression. "You need a walk, darlin'. Why don't you go get her something soft and cuddly? Gift shop is probably closed this time of night so you'll have to go to the convenience store 'bout a block east from here, m'kay?" She pats my shoulder and disappears before I can respond.

Soft and cuddly. Yeah, I can do that. I pivot and head in the general direction I recall Liam coming from earlier. This hospital is huge, someone could easily get lost in here. My surroundings blur together as I absentmindedly wander down the empty hall. Turning a corner, I spot a guy a little taller than me with tattoos peeking up his neck from under his worn leather jacket. Would I have ended up like him if life had gone differently? He's carrying a bouquet of peach roses and his riding pants have definitely met the asphalt more than once. I wonder who he is here for? Mom, grandma? A wife, maybe? Nah, a guy like him wouldn't be held down like that. He meets my gaze and shoots one of those polite smiles that acknowledges you're a person but doesn't invite conversation as he passes. That's the kind of guy I thought I was when we were younger. Too cool, invincible, rugged and mean-looking. Now I can't even handle sitting with my girl while she recovers from damage I helped cause without wanting to puke on my shoes. Fuck, maybe that guy wants to puke too.

Somehow, I've gone in a big circle and see the nurses station up ahead. The guy is talking quietly to a bubbly blonde who is practically bouncing on her toes under his attention. I keep my head down as I pass, I'm sure it looks fucking suspicious for me to be lapping the floor again.

"No, I understand. She is probably asleep anyway. Could you just pass these along to her for me?" I overhear him asking the nurse as I pass. I wonder when normal visiting hours ended if he isn't allowed to hand deliver the flowers to whoever he is here for. I guess we get special treatment since Elsie has a different circumstance. He falls into step not far behind me and I hear him chuckle.

"You work at that shop over off NASA right?" He

strikes up a conversation. *Shit, I hate dealing with customers.*

"Uh, yeah." I slow so he can catch up. Pointing to his pants I smirk, "Your bike need some work?"

"No, no it takes the falls better than I do." He chuckles. Man, he has a strangely deep voice. "You guys did some work for a buddy of mine not too long ago and I've got a civic that needs to be looked at but I saw the shop was closed today. I hope everything is alright." *This guy drives a civic? Must be suped up.*

"Yeah, family emergency. I hope whoever you're here for is okay…" I trail off, hoping he'll tell me about his sick grandmother or something.

"Girl friend." He says with a nod. "Anyway, I guess I'll bring it by the shop next week or something." I nod as we part ways and I continue around the damn circle again. Where the fuck are the elevators?

The 'someone' in my previous thought about getting lost in this place being me apparently as I pass the nurses station for a third time. I think I am starting to worry the employees so I decide to crawl out of my head for a second and focus. Looking for signs, I see that straight ahead should be the elevators. I follow down the hall again but this time taking in the stupid motivational posters and each room number I pass. The shiny metal doors finally catch my eye in an alcove to my left and I veer toward them.

Smashing the down arrow, I tap my foot impatiently. Now that I've found the damned things it's like my skin is too tight and sweat streams down my back. I need to get outside. That's all. I just need some air.

Chapter 11

Liam
Present day

Rhett's sudden exit leaves me anxious, making my stomach churn but I paste on a reassuring smile for Elsie and brush a few strands of hair back from her forehead. She doesn't flinch away, just stares at the corner that conceals the doorway from her view.

"We could've used the call button…" she mumbles. I nod and stroke her hand quietly. There is no point in replying right now, she can't hear me anyway. Trying to explain that the strong, hot-headed delinquent she had known has been reduced to an anxiety filled, self-loathing husk of a man over text message is just not my idea of fun. Theo bobs his head as well and gives her a lopsided smile with an eye roll - as if they have some kind of silent inside joke already. She blushes slightly and looks down at our hands.

"What was that?" I ask Theo in a light tone.

"Nothing, just trying to communicate to her that I think his reaction is a bit ridiculous too." He shrugs like it's no big deal. Luckily, his answer is innocent enough and the insecurity squeezing my heart loosens again. I have never been the jealous type, not even when it came to Elsie. I guess because I had always shared her affections with Rhett and since I'd lived through all of her relationships on the side lines just hoping that waiting patiently enough would bring her around to me someday. But something about losing her has apparently made me possessive and jealous over even the most simple of interactions. I am definitely going to need to keep a lid on that. *Shit, if I feel like this Rhett must be feeling it worse.*

"Officer? Do you have a moment?" Rebekah asks from the door, gesturing that they should step into the hallway.

"Uh, yeah." He squeezes Elsies foot gently while giving me a quizzical look before heading to see what the nurse could possibly need.

"I'm sure it's nothing." I tell Elsie even though I know she can't hear well. She chews her bottom lip nervously and an ache forms in my chest unsure how to help her. I wish I could just wrap her up and take all the pain away. Pulling out my phone, I tap her hand gently to draw her attention away from her worries.

L: We own a mechanic shop together and share an apartment. We go by Rhett (mason) and Liam now. We were or are in a witness program.

I show her the text and closely watch her face as she absorbs this new information. It occurs to me that she likely knows nothing about the circumstances of her kidnapping and I'm not sure how much to tell her. She tenderly grasps my phone and awkwardly taps out her reply.

E: I'll live with you two right? Did you pick those names yourself?

L: Yes, that's the plan. I wish but they were assigned to us.

E: They fit you both. Do I have to use those names or can I still call you Milo?

L: For everyone's safety, it's better if we use the new names. I think you will get to pick out a new identity too if you want. Is there anyone who you think you might need to hide from?

I wait patiently for her to take the phone back like she had been but instead she looks away. Frowning, I start to tap out a text to say she doesn't have to tell me when without warning her little hand snatches my phone out of my grasp. I catch her wrist just before she can throw it across the room. Her monitors beep loudly as alarms sound her distress. She thrashes against me, trying to rip her wrist from my grip. For a moment, I'm torn on what to do. Let her go and have her possibly injure herself more in her panic or hold her tighter and restrain her until she calms down. Or passes out. It's always a split second decision with these things.

I catch sight of her other hand darting towards the wiring and tubes she is hooked up to and my mind is made up. In a practiced motion, I grip her other wrist and slide onto the bed behind her holding her arms crossed over her chest. She rears back attempting to head butt me but she only manages to bump my chest. Holding her steady while she fights and cries is much easier than when Rhett has a meltdown but no less heart wrenching. *Thank god Rhett isn't here to see this.*

Rebekah and Theo fumble over each other in their rush to get in the room and both stand still for a moment looking a little stunned at our position. Theo approaches with his hands palms up in front of him and tries to catch her eyes. She wails and crunches her eyes closed as she bucks against my iron clad hold.

"Get a sedative." I order and the nurse darts back into the hallway for just a moment before returning with a syringe. I wrap my legs around Elsies lower half and hold her as still as possible while Rebekah quickly injects the medication into her IV.

"NONONONONO! NO!Please...please..." Elsie's

cries begin to trail off as the sedative takes effect and her muscles soften. Loosening my grip on her, I carefully reposition us so she is laid on her side and I'm pressed against her back with an arm over her middle securing her to me.

"It's okay. Shhh. It's okay." I whisper the words into the hair on the back of her head as she fades back off to sleep.

"What happened?" Theo asks, keeping his tone even. He isn't accusing me of some wrongdoing just yet.

"Here, we were texting. I didn't think that question would set her off, I'll be more careful." I hand him my phone from where I'd stashed it on her bed with the text thread open. He reads it quickly before releasing a heavy sigh and nodding. I'm vaguely aware of Rebekah flitting around the room resetting alarms, logging information into a computer and checking screens. A blonde nurse practically skips into the room, looking way too happy for the situation that just occurred. She is carrying a bouquet of peach roses and I sigh. Rhett must have sent her with them I guess while he continues to clear his head. *Where'd he get flowers anyway? It's after visiting hours - there's no way the gift shop is open. Do they even sell flowers?*

"Ope, awkward..." The blonde chirps interrupting my thoughts as she takes in my possessive position on the bed with El.

"Steph, I told you to keep those out there." Rebekah grits out between clenched teeth. "We don't know who that man was." If looks could kill, Rebekah would be on murder trial for Steph's untimely demise.

"He said he was her boyfriend... one of them, anyway, I guess." She chortles at her own distasteful joke with a hair flip punctuated by a hand on the hip.

"What man?" I question, subconsciously tightening my arm around Elsie.

"That's why we stepped out..." Theo starts to explain.

"A tatted hottie in leather." Steph smirks as she talks over him.

"It wasn't Rhett." Rebekah replies at the same time. Adrenaline attempts to cloud my judgment before I push it down and focus on Theo. His face is a rigid frown aimed at Steph. *He doesn't just dislike her - he doesn't trust her.*

"Give me those." Rebekah snaps at Steph as she snatches the flowers. "Out." She orders and thankfully Steph leaves with one last glance tossed over her shoulder.

"Is there a card?" I ask. Theo nods before pulling it from his pocket, already in a little ziploc bag for evidence. He holds it close enough for me to be able to read the handwritten note.

Only the best for you my love. A rose for each hour they've kept you from me.

You are mine. I promise.

• R

Chapter 12

Elsie
Present Day

"Kelly will stay here with you all while she wakes up and becomes oriented to her surroundings again. If you all have any questions, don't hesitate to ask." A strange man's voice filters in through the haze like I've got cotton stuffed in my ears.

"It won't be long now." A warm, feminine voice says. Feeling creeps back into my consciousness slowly starting as a tingle in my toes. My arms and head feel heavy. *I know this feeling, I've been drugged again.* I lay quietly allowing awareness to dance in and out while my ears to try and pinpoint where Reaper is. He is never far away when I wake up like this. If it wasn't for his exploitation of me, he'd almost seem sweet in these moments. He'll prop my head up and insist I only take small sips of water through a straw before hand feeding me tiny heart shaped sandwiches. It is during those times that he admits any remorse for his hand in my undoing. Once he even confessed that if he was capable of love, he'd love me the most.

I have almost come to look forward to this time with him. Almost because no matter how sweet or tenderly he treats me now, he will issue punishment for whatever I did to need to be drugged in the first place. I usually won't remember the reason until he is slowly describing in detail how my indiscretion cost him somehow and that I need to pay him back for his kindness in preventing me from making a situation worse. A shudder rolls over my body and my eyes pop open. *He is a busy man.*

I'm in a white walled room with harsh fluorescent lighting. I blink several times as confusion washes over me. Three men are standing at the foot of the bed I am in, all vaguely familiar to me but none of them are Reaper. *Oh god, did he sell me? Did he get sick of me? What have I done?* Tears prick my eyes and panic replaces the confusion. A smiling older woman with graying hair and wrinkles pokes her head in front of my face.

"There you are, dear! You are at Loveland Hospital in Houston Texas. You're recovering from some serious injuries. You had surgery a few days ago, how is your hearing? Any pain?" She inquires and I shake my head without really taking stock. *How the hell did I get here?* "I need some words, honey." She encourages with a smile still blocking the potential threats at the foot of the bed with her too cheery face.

"I am okay." I tell her quietly. She beams at me and finally sits up, I don't bother watching her to see what she is up to. My eyes bounce between the three men at the end of my bed and memories try to tickle my brain. One of them has a police uniform on, he is standing off to the left. His hair is buzzed short and his stance is relaxed as he assesses me. He must be overseeing this trade. *Dirty fucking cops.* The man in the middle is the largest by several inches. He has a few tattoos on his arms and looks a bit scruffy. His blood shot eyes telling me he is probably on something, which would make him the hired help in case there are any issues. That makes the pretty boy at the end the most likely buyer. He isn't any less built than the other two though and my chances of escaping this new hell shrink.

"Here sip on this." The woman, *Kelly*, instructs while jabbing a cold cup into my hands. I instinctively grab it. Internally, I yearn for Reaper's kind touches and care as the three men just stare at me while I bring the straw to my lips. *Best to be obedient for now. I can't believe he fucking sold me. Lying Bastard.*

"Elsie, do you remember what happened last time you were awake?" The Officer asks me.

"I…I'm not sure." I admit, a little shocked he is using my real name.

"What is the last thing you remember?" He presses. *Am I supposed to remember how I got here or not? Is there a right answer?* Damn it, after all these years I thought I'd be better at this. To be fair, I had only been sold a handful of times before Reaper collected me and I had been with him for years. I was out of practice.

"Um…Reaper was … making me beautiful." I answer carefully, though honestly. Last I recall Reaper had me face down in a storage container at some ship port. He was doing one of his roped masterpieces. Memories of the sweet mutterings of his praise in my ear makes my heart throb for a more familiar reality than this.

"Fuck." The largest man turns away and looks up at the ceiling. I guess I wasn't supposed to remember. Pretty boy touches his shoulder in a reassuring manner and smiles softly at me.

"Elsie, you were found during a police raid in a shipping container at Port Padre about two weeks ago. We believe you are a victim of sex trafficking. Does that sound correct to you?" The Officer continues his questioning clinically and I blink.

"I was…found?" My voice breaks as tears threaten to drip down my face. *He hadn't sold me. I had been… found.*

"Yes, Elsie. You are safe here. Were you a victim of sex trafficking?"

"Yes." I bob my head frantically as the truth of his statement pings some part of my brain that had never given up hope on being rescued.

"Okay. Elsie, before we go any further I'd like to know if you recognize me or either of these two men?" The Officer gestures to the men beside him and the large man in the middle turns to look at me, gripping the rail at the bottom of my bed for support. With a new perspective, I study each of them as familiarity turns to pin pricks in my brain. I take another sip of juice to buy myself sometime.

"Are you sure you'll be okay?" Milo's face pokes in between the front seats to look at me for the millionth time. I roll my eyes at his pretty blue ones and stupid blonde hair. Why do my friends have to be so hot and sweet?

"That's Milo and that's Mason." I point at each of them as reality hits me square in the chest and a sob breaks free. Matching smiles transform these men into their younger selves. Holy shit, I'd been found! The memories have started pouring back now and I nod as I look at the cop. "You're the one who found me." I state confidently and he grins at me in relief.

"That's correct, Elsie. Do you recall waking up in the hospital prior to this at all? It's okay if you don't." He has stepped closer to the bed now. Mason has come to sit in a hard chair next to me and he reaches out for me. I instinctively grab his hand and squeeze twice like we used to do all the time.

"Uh…no I don't, I'm sorry." I stare at Milo in amazement. He looks like his mom; how could I have ever mistaken him for some criminal?

"That's alright. The doctors have kept you sedated for your own safety. The last few times you've woken up haven't gone so well." He grimaces before continuing. "You are ready for discharge as soon as Ms. Kelly here gives us the green light. Would you like to go to Mason and Milo's home while we talk more?" I take a deep breath. My eyes searching the space again and nerves filling my stomach. *He didn't sell me.*

"Um…yeah, okay." I nod as I fidget.

"Oh goody! I've got some clothes for you here; we are so happy you're going home." Kelly beams as she unhooks me from the blood pressure cuff and finger clippy thing. She hands me some baby pink sweats with a wink. "These men have been doing their best to spoil you, I already had them take the blankets and all out to the car. Alright you three, go wait in the hall while she gets dressed. No need to drag this out when I can make lunch on time. You shouldn't need any help but if you do just press that red button, okay?" I barely nod before she stands and ushers everyone out of the room. I grip the soft material in my hands tightly and just take in the silence for a moment before sliding out of bed. I pull the string at the nape of my neck and the gown flutters to the floor with a quick shake. Pretty shades of blues, purples, greens and yellows decorate my skin as they have for years and I cling to that notion. That hasn't changed just yet.

Reaper told me often how beautiful of a canvas I am for him. The rope burns that usually make my skin tender have healed without a trace and I sigh. Pulling the hoodie over my head, I find a matching pair of Hanes cotton panties nestled between them along with some socks. Stepping into the underwear and feeling the comfortable fabric cradle me securely feels foreign after so long of being without any clothing but especially underwear. If I was good, Reaper would let me wear the fancy dresses he likes to buy and he'd take me to dinner but I was never allowed any under garments. Never allowed to speak to anyone or use the restroom while we were there. He'd play happy doting husband and I'd fill the role of his meek, docile trophy wife.

After a while, it was a comfortable role and I kind of wish he was here in a way. My stomach churns and my heart squeezes at the thought. Quickly, pulling on my pants and shoving my feet into the socks I flee the room. *The further I get from that life the easier it will be to forget Him.*

Chapter 13

Rhett
Present Day

I know I'm hovering but I can't fucking stop. Elsie is standing in our empty apartment for the first time as Liam tries to explain the state of it to her and Theo as if he can reason away why either of us felt like making it homier was a betrayal somehow.

"So, you know, we just never really got around to it. Least it's easy to keep clean though." He half jokes with a smile that I'm sure would've dazzled a younger El. Instead her eyes are glazed as she looks around as if she isn't really here at all. "We will make it better Elsie, I promise. You can decorate it…"

"It's fine." She says quietly as he trails off and Theo shifts nervously watching the exchange. *Damn it, this is not going well.* I step closer in behind her and she takes me by surprise when she steps back into me, leaning lightly on my chest with her arms folded. She looks exhausted - not like she needs more sleep but as if all the light of her personality has been bled out of her. Her soul is screaming for a sense peace and comfort I no longer know how to offer her.

"Let's get some food delivered, yeah? And you can look at some furniture and stuff on my phone?" I offer her gently. She jolts away from me and whirls around, her expression momentarily confused like she was expecting to see someone else. She takes a big gulp of air and fidgets with her fingers as she creeps further into the apartment.

"It's fine. Really." She insists quietly as she retreats to the far corner. She lowers herself cautiously on to the floor with her back to the wall. *Fuck she is so scared.* I can see her chest heaving from here. I follow and slide down the wall to sit near her and give her a small smile. "Mason, it's fine. I don't mind the apartment." She reassures again.

"Well, I do." Supplies Theo. God I could deck him right now for that. "You need a bed. I need a couch to sleep on and a TV wouldn't hurt guys." He rolls his eyes as he grunts and groans to fold himself onto the floor across from us. "You want some tacos…what is your stomach feeling up to?" He inquires of Elsie. I watch as she mauls her lip, her eyes tracking Liam who paces nearby.

"How about soup, hmm?" Liam asks without pause as he pulls up his phone. He doesn't wait for an answer, taking charge and I see her relax just a little as he continues. "Panera has a really good broccoli one you will love. They also have this mango lemonade that will blow your mind if you let it." He chuckles and hands me the phone. I tap in my order quickly, constantly glancing over to check on her. To confirm she really is here in my living room. *We really need a couch, she looks so uncomfortable curled in on herself on the floor.* I hand the phone off to Theo and it crosses my mind like a whisper how quickly he became one of us. Only days ago we had formed some kind of weird crime-fighting villain-hunting squad bonding us for eternity. Even if I still kind of hate the guy. *Anything for my peach.* "I'm thinking we can get one of those cloud sectionals, in a dark green I think. And put a book case right there." Liam continues on, the cadence of his voice effectively laying a blanket of comfort over both me and Elsie. "We have a good sized bed right now but as soon as we get lunch on the way I'll look and see what same day delivery we can get for furniture. Maybe an air mattress for you Theo." He adds jokingly.

"Ha ha. Yeah something to sleep on without having to become Rhett's newest stuffed animal would be great. A blanket too." Theo laughs and Elsie lets out the smallest chuckle at their banter.

"You got it, man. For reference though, I am the only human getting intense Rhett snuggles currently." He says with a gleam to his smile and a wink at El who just shakes her head slightly. "I should order some groceries too. Oh shoot, office supply refill while I'm at it." He muses as he gets his phone back from Theo. Presumably he is absorbed with becoming an interior designer because he shuts up and wanders off, leaving us to fall into a charged silence.

I watch Elsie closely as the minutes stretch on. She is staring at the front door intently. *Does she want to leave?* Maybe she hates how small it is.

"I could take you to go see the shop downstairs…" I offer her but she shakes her head without looking at me. Drumming my fingers on the floor, I try again. Maybe my voice will comfort her like Liam's does for me when I'm feeling off. "We didn't get to keep much of your things. I have your remember me box though."

"You do?" She perks up and stares at me. "You aren't allowed to talk about it." She adds as she looks back at the door.

"Do you want to see it? Gotta be honest with you babe, I've looked at everything in there." I chuckle and rub at the back of my neck. "I know I wasn't supposed to but it was the only thing we really had time to grab when everything went down." I shrug. I wish she would just look at anything but that door.

"Whats a remember me box?" Theo butts in.

"It's filled with the stuff she felt was important. A memory box." I shrug while standing to go get it.

"No." She says, her focus elsewhere.

"Okay." I nod and sit back down a little perplexed. I thought she'd want it back as soon as possible. "Maybe later then."

"No." She repeats in that same vacant tone.

"Why not? You loved that box, it was everything you ever needed remember?" I smile, trying to pull her into the present with me. Where the hell is Liam anyway? He is probably better suited to help her right now.

"I'm not the same girl anymore, Mason." She says with a small glance at me before looking to the door again.

"Who are you then?" I ask quietly. I know I'm not the same anymore either and I pray with a burning passion that who we are now is as in sync as we were before. She stares at the door for so long that we all jump when a knock sounds from the other side. Theo stands to answer it, hand on his holster just incase it isn't our lunch.

Too fast to stop, Elsie bolts ahead of Theo and throws the door open. She stumbles out onto the small porch area as me and Theo yell for her to stop. Liam must've heard the commotion though because he somehow reaches her before I do. I can't see around fucking Theo. I grumble internally as

I shoulder him backwards with a glare. He glares back at me but heads to where we had all been sitting moments ago. Elsie is standing just outside our front door looking down at the brown paper bag as she sniffles.

"It's okay, El. It's just lunch." Liam calmly reaches around her and hands me the bag of food without looking back at me. It smells delicious.

"I just…I thought…Maybe…" She sniffles and her gaze searches the parking lot below. She looks heart broken.

"What Elsie? Who did you think it was?" Liam asks as he slowly inches closer to her. She doesn't say anything for a long moment and I can see how tense Liam is that she might do something stupid. I set lunch down in case he needs back up.

"My parents. I thought it would be them." She states lamely, the lie obvious to me. But why lie about that? Who had she really thought would come looking for her? Liam gently wraps an arm around her shoulders and guides her inside.

"Okay." He states calmly. As soon as they are inside again I close the door and follow behind after grabbing the food again. I watch as Liam folds himself onto the floor nearby Theo and stares up at her. "What do you need?" He asks and she just shakes her head. "Sit back down where you were." He instructs her and I watch from behind as her head bobs and she moves back to the corner. When she turns to face me, kneeling this time I see the tears rolling down her cheeks to her neck. I flop down less gracefully and she jumps a little. I ignore it. I can't take the way she watches us, like we're the people she needs saving from. And the lying? Already?

I hand out food to the guys and then grasp her soup in my hand, scooting closer. I fill the plastic spoon with soup wordlessly and she opens her mouth obediently. I slowly calm down as I feed her and the action seems to have the same effect on her as her tears dry and breathing evens out.

I've got you.

Chapter 14

Liam
Present Day

Watching Rhett feed her, I choke down my lunch. I'm not even sure what I ordered and definitely don't taste it. I kind of hate Panera, but Elsie seems to be enjoying it. And honestly, I don't know where else we could've gotten soup delivered from. I should have thought ahead and had groceries delivered before she was discharged. Furniture too. Oh well, too late to change any of that now.

"Thanks for lunch, it was really good." Theo says giving the room a segway.

"Yeah, I really like their steak sandwich." Rhett replies. It surprises me a little that he responded at all being he is now pressing the straw to his lemonade to Elsie's lips. I'd chide him for being so intense with her but somehow they seem to have regulated each other in their own weird way.

"I haven't tried that one. Maybe we can order in

dinner from there too? My treat." Theo is a good balance for us. Adding in the casualness me and Rhett are usually missing.

"Hear that? More soup for dinner, babe." Rhett prods at her lips with the spoon and she opens for him quietly.

"So, I picked out a couch that can be rearranged pretty easily. I was thinking you could sleep on that Theo? It gets the size of a king when set up correctly I think." I turn my attention away from Rhett and Elsie. Something about their interaction is making my dick hard even though I know how utterly wrong and sick that is considering what she just got out of.

"Okay. You got some extra bedding too? Where's she going to sleep?" Theo's reply thoroughly distracts me.

"I was just about to ask her but…anyway, I've got a twin mattress on the way too that we can set up somewhere." He nods at my reply as he eyes the pair of them and adjusts himself. So, I'm not the only one having impure thoughts huh?

"Good job." Rhett tells Elsie and she flutters her eyes at him wordlessly. "Let's go to bed." He states confidently and she stands without question.

"Wait, guys we need to talk about that." Theo says standing too.

"No, we don't. She ate, she is tired. It's time for a

nap." Rhett glares daggers at Theo as he gently pulls Elsie along behind him, heading towards the bed room. Theo opens his mouth to argue but I silence him with a hand on his shoulder.

"Let them go. Probably better she is sleeping or at least tucked safely away when the other deliveries start showing up. He won't hurt her."

"He can't treat her like that. She needs to find her independence." He argues quietly. He isn't wrong.

"It's her first day out in the world again. She has time to find it but for now I'm thinking she needs a day or two of still being told what to do and when. I'm guessing she didn't get much say over her life. Coming back to being in control can be overwhelming." I explain quietly as I settle back on to the floor. Theo huffs and looks down at me.

"Should you go supervise or something? He isn't exactly stable…" Theo looks like he'd like to go supervise himself if I'm being honest. Just an assignment, right?

"No, I trust him. They're going to take a nap not diffuse a bomb." I chuckle at his intensity. "When did it become more than an assignment?"

"What? It's not!" He looks completely taken by surprise and then rolls his eyes. "I've got a hero complex okay? She is all distressed damsel and I just want to keep her safe." I grunt and shake my head at him. "When's the stuff getting here? Your floor is really uncomfortable."

"In a few hours." I eye the mess from lunch and internally groan. Rhett has always been a bit of a slob but I don't mind too much generally. I start collecting trash and give Theo a nod of thanks as he begins to do the same. I stretch and glance around awkwardly since our task too little time.

"You know, if you had a TV we could've watched something instead of standing around staring at each other." Theo smiles and I laugh.

"Yeah, yeah. It's coming!"

"How're you handling all this? Seems like you already had one charge, taking on another one who is so… well…it just seems like a lot for anyone." He tucks his hands in his front pockets and rocks on his heels as he stares at me. It's a loaded question for sure but I blow out a huff of air.

"Well they're safe, fed and hopefully sleeping so I'm doing an alright job." He chuckles and bobs his head as I continue. "Who do you think she was looking for out there?"

"Probably the guy that came looking for her at the hospital. I really need to get a statement from her as soon as possible." I nod and glance at the door again.

"He isn't just going to give up. Tell me you guys have some kind of a plan." I grimace as he puts on his best cop face.

"We do. We believe he would've followed us from the hospital and have patrol cars nearby to keep everyone secure. As soon as he shows his face, we will have him in cuffs to find out exactly what he had to with Elsie and the others we found at the port." He looks confident enough but something about this whole situation doesn't sit right.

"He has to be bad news but... why would she go looking for him if he had hurt her?" I muse, perplexed.

"I don't know. Maybe we have it wrong and he was some kind of good guy trying to find a way out for both of them. Its just has hard to get out of the trade as a dealer." He shrugs and checks his phone. "Something tells me that isn't the case though."

"You're a good cop. We'll see if she is up for a statement over dinner." I offer.

"That'd be good. At least we have his street name now – presumably anyway. Reaper." He scoffs and rolls his eyes.

"Yeah, how original. Makes me wonder if he started off as a hitman or something." Theo just stares back at me blankly. "You know, cause then he could've earned the nickname – like the Grim Reaper? Brings death wherever he goes?" He stares at me for several more seconds in silence but he starts laughing. Full bellied laughing at me. I start laughing and before long we are both hysterically howling with laughter. It's not funny. I know that but something about this whole fucked up situation is so surreal its hard not to laugh.

"Hey!" A whisper shout from the bed room dulls us to a chuckle as we direct our attention to Rhett, who is standing in the doorway looking murderous. We all freeze for a moment before we start snickering again. "Damn it, shut up! She just fell asleep." He is barely retaining his own laugh now and that just serves to make us chortle louder.

Chapter 15

Elsie
Present Day

It takes me a moment to orient myself to my surroundings again when I wake up. I'm alone and someone is speaking too loudly in the living room. It must be the deliveries of furniture and food and god knows what else Milo might have thought to order because I don't know the voice. I cringe thinking about the amount of money he probably just spent in hopes I'd feel more *at home*. I don't think I'll ever feel at home again without Reaper and that thought sends shivers down my spine. I hadn't thought I'd miss him. I used to daydream of being rescued and brought back to see my parents, my best friends and how freeing that would be. I could go to college and start my life again away from all the heinous, violent acts hiding in the shadows where men and women alike fulfill their darkest desires. But now that freedom is a reality, all I want is to return to what I know is a safe-ish option. The guys can't protect me like he can. They haven't seen the things I have. They don't even know me anymore. I'm dirty, soiled by the depravity in this world.

I can't unsee Lilahs thousand yard stare as they took turns breaking her bones. I'll never be able to remove the memory of the sound her body made when they raped her over and over again once she was nothing but a skin bag of mush. I'll always know the way the drugs made my stomach churn as I lay on that dirty floor with a never ending stream of men and women using me. Like I wasn't a person anymore. Reaper was like an avenging angel that night he pulled back the curtain to reveal my dirty, beaten body. He stood over me with those bright blue eyes, his nose slightly scrunched from the smell and he'd snarled something that summoned the man that'd put me there weeks or maybe it was months prior. Then, I was floating through the makeshift halls of that dreadful building while Reaper whispered sweet nothings.

I know he isn't a good man but he had been good to me, right? *He had saved me.* The last several years the only thing that I've been able to believe and hold on for certain was that I belonged to him. That I was his treasure and he would never be without me. I know that he is a powerful man - I've seen first hand the kinds of things he can make happen with a flick of his wrist - so why hasn't he come for me? I sit up in bed and really take in the room. It's plain. Empty save for the bed I'm in. The comforter is a navy blue and clearly well worn - the sheets and flat pillows match. It strikes me how different Mason and Milo are now. Even as kids they both enjoyed decorating their spaces and the luxuries of comfort items.

Reaper had enjoyed the finer things in life too. I sigh, the feeling of missing him deeply rooted in my soul becoming almost a physical ache in my chest. Rationally, I should hate him but I don't. I think at some point he had begun to look less like my captor and more like a savior. I endured such horrible, cruel things before he claimed me and honestly I'd gotten off easy compared to some of the poor souls I met. Once I was his though - I was only *touched* by him. Viewed by many but only he was allowed to touch me.

He was gentle with me unless I forgot my place or angered him. He hand fed me often and showered me in compliments. I wasn't a toy to him. I was a canvas just waiting for him to turn into a masterpiece. A work of art. I shake my head to clear the thoughts of admiration.

God, what the hell is wrong with me? He bound me, controlled every part of my life and used me against my will! I shouldn't be sitting here - in my best friend's bed - thinking about all the silver linings of being with Reaper. Who is a fucking criminal! I don't need to romanticize him anymore. I'm free. I'm with Milo and Mason now. *But you know where all the bad men play*, a small annoying voice in my head reminds me.

Deciding I need to get out of my head before I start really talking to myself, I gently stand and head for the living area where I can still hear talking and furniture being moved about. I open the door slowly and peek out. Milo is directing traffic of about a dozen guys hauling pieces of a huge couch, side table, book shelves - is that a giant bean bag? I stifle my laugh and let my eyes seek out Mason. He is leaning against the wall by the front door acting as a door prop as he studies each of the men as they enter and exit the apartment. Theo appears to be missing for the moment and I take a deep breath of relief. I'm not ready to talk yet and I am sure that's exactly what he is hanging around for.

Stepping slightly more into the threshold, I'm happy to have not been spotted in the chaos just yet when I lock eyes with a familiar pair of sapphire ones and my breathing stops. Short dark hair, hulking frame and... a rooms to go uniform? I blink not certain if I'm imagining Reaper moving furniture pieces around the room or not but he smirks and places one finger to his lips. *Be Quiet.* I bite my lower lip and avert my eyes to look at Mason who is glaring at one of the other employees.

He had come back for me. He hadn't abandoned me after all. I don't know if I should be terrified or delighted in this moment. My body feels numb, surreal like I am in a dream state of sorts aside from the pounding of my heart strumming in my ears. My eyes trail back to Reaper and he finishes positioning a book case in the corner I had been sitting in only hours ago. Did he know that? Had he been watching this entire time?

"Hey man, I wanted that on the other side of the room." Milo instructs Reaper. They don't know. Oh god, there's a murderous bastard in our living room and Milo just told him to move the damn book case again! To his credit, Reaper just nods and then shoots me a wink. That catches Mason's attention and he spins to face me. "Elsie, I'm sorry we didn't mean to wake you."

"It's fine." My eyes ping pong between him, Mason and Reaper. Reaper smirks at me with a pointed look. Mason leaves his post by the door to come to me and Reaper strolls right out the front door behind him. *Completely undetected.* My eyes follow him until he is out of sight and Mason is standing right in front of me.

"You okay?" Milo inquires with a furrowed brow. Swallowing hard, I paste on a smile for them.

"Yes, I'm okay." For the first time since I woke up, I think it might actually be true. "What did you buy?" I redirect their attention and only half listen as they begin a tour of all their new things. *Their new things.* Because in that moment I know I can't stay - not when every fiber of my being is willing me to run out the door and throw myself into Reapers waiting embrace. *He came back for me. I am His.*

No matter how fucked up that is.

Chapter 16

Rhett
Present Day

I grunt as Liam nonchalantly elbows me in the side. I don't even need to fucking look at him to know why either- he wants me to back off Elsie. Well too fucking bad for him cause I can tell something is wrong with our girl. She hasn't mentioned the incident earlier and I'm just waiting for a moment to bring it up without upsetting her. She was already crestfallen when Theo showed back up and asked her if she was ready to submit a statement.

Now I'm sitting on the new couch staring holes into the side of her head - hence Liam's irritation. Theo is sitting on a tall backed chair that seems a little out of place in our now crowded apartment with a notepad and pen; what was he thinking ordering all this stuff?

"Elsie, I had a recorder with me and I'll be recording this session," Theo states and pauses for Elsie's nod before continuing. "It is our understanding you were abducted approximately seven years ago and the details are unknown leading up to discovering you, a car and several other victims in a unit recently. Please in your own words tell me what happened?"

We all wait quietly while she stares down at her fidgeting fingers; I'm not sure why hearing what happened to her is so important to me since she is home now but it's like a hive of angry bees has taken up residence in my stomach and sweat coats my palms. I know it was bad *but how bad?* What memories torment her? What does she know about how things went down?

"Where do I start?" She finally asks in a tiny voice, barely above a whisper.

"At the very beginning." Theo instructs as he moves his tape recorder closer to her. I watch closely as she takes a steadying breath.

"I wasn't feeling good, so I was laying down in the back of Mason's car while the guys went in the store...I don't even remember what they were supposed to be getting." She shakes her head and rolls her shoulders back uncomfortably. I wish I could take that discomfort and punch it in the face.

"And then what happened?" Theo prompts after she is quiet for too long.

"Uh, well... I heard a noise just about side the car

and I sat up to look outside. Jett was there and he was messing with the back window. It was tinted so dark I knew he couldn't see me but he knew whose car it was. I don't know if he was planning to steal it or what..." She shakes her head.

"And who was Jett to you?" Theo inquiries professionally. My blood boils just thinking about that lowlife weasel.

"He was my ex-boyfriend. We dated on and off for a while but I stopped seeing him when he got too rough one time." She swallows and glances up at me. She had never gone back to Jett after that day we kissed - in fact she didn't have another boyfriend at all. "Anyway, I opened the door and he jumped back surprised. He kind of just stood there for a second before asking me why I was in the car to which I'd asked what he was doing to the car and we just sorta stared at each other in silence but then I heard a man shouting at him. He sounded really angry." She shudders at the thought and I know exactly who she would've been hearing; *Bullet.* I'm not surprised he scared her, he was one intimidating dude. "He had a bald head aaaaaaaaaaaand was white?" She pauses as she waits for Theo to nod at her to continue. "He shoved Jett and was yelling at him about touching other people's property. I should've just closed the door but... I didn't want Jett to get hurt so I got out and got between them. I was trying to stop their fighting but Jett was a hothead too. Next thing I knew I was staring down the barrel of a gun." She swallows thickly. She's lost in a daze she recalls the moments leading up to her kidnapping. "It was the first gun I'd ever seen in real life but there was no mistaking it. I'll never forget how loud it was. I thought I'd died for a second. He'd shot Jett and everything else just seemed so surreal. I remember lunging like I'd be able to wrestle the gun away or something but he hit me in the head and that's all I remember until..." She trails off as she curls into herself.

"Until what?" Theo prods and for once I'm thankful for him because I'm on the edge of my seat listening. She hadn't told us much that we didn't know except the motive behind it all. *Fucking Jett.*

"I...I woke up tied to a chair." She glances up at Theo before studying the arm of the new couch like it's the most interesting thing in the world. He waits and eventually, she sighs. "I was naked and they'd tied my arms behind me to the back of the chair and my knees and ankles to the front legs. I don't know where we were but the bald guy was there along with at least six other men. They were drinking, laughing and t-talking about whether they should take t-turns with me before I *go.* I thought they meant *go home...*" I think I'm going to be sick. I bolt from the couch and barely make it to the toilet in time to hurl as that thought registers. Bullet had wasted no time stripping her down and treating her like an object. Bullet who had been protecting *my* shit and probably thought he was doing *me* a solid. A warm hand rubs my back and a cool cloth finds my forehead. Liam is always there to save the fucking day.

"How about you go lay down? We can finish it without you." His voice is full of concern but he has no idea how much I'm welcoming the shame, guilt and self-hatred listening to her is bringing on. She lived it - the least I can fucking do is listen to her story.

"No. I need to hear this. I want to be there to support her. I'll get my shit together." I nod encouragingly as I stand to rinse my mouth. I know he doesn't believe me but *what the hells he gonna do about? Not a damn thing.*

"…They had buyers inspect me before I'd woken up apparently and were just waiting for the highest bidder to show up." Her sweet voice floats through to the apartment and I do my best to keep my composure. Liam scoffs and turns to find his seat on the couch again. I'm two steps behind him and had I not seen his tightly fisted hand he might've been able to convince everyone he wasn't bothered by her words - but that vice grip says otherwise.

Chapter 17

Liam
Present Day

Elsie's recount of the ordeal makes me equally angry and disgusted that such excuses for humans exist. The majority of them are probably still out there doing this to other people as well. I repress a shudder as I return to her side. I'm certain this is just the tip of the iceberg of horrors as I study her solemn expression.

"Do I have to say what happened next?" Her voice cracks and my heart aches for her.

"We can take a break. Maybe it'll be better for everyone if we do this in a different setting, with some other professionals." Theo nods to himself as he cuts the recorder off and jots down some more notes. "I understand this is difficult for you, Elsie."

"You mean a shrink." She scoffs. "I'm not crazy, I'm just …I've just seen …things." The emphasis on the last word sends a tingle over my skin. She hadn't just seen them she'd experienced it first hand.

"I mean that you've been through quite a lot and could use some support that isn't personally tied to you." Theo keeps his tone light, professional, and detached.

"Quite a lot..." she whispers as she rolls her eyes. "You're just guessing. You have no idea what my life has been like - tell me Officer have you watched someone you considered a friend burned with acid until she couldn't scream anymore and then sliced apart so they could sell what organs they hadn't destroyed yet? Huh?" She's not yelling yet but the pain and rage are evident in her tone. I scoot a little closer as I recall her last outburst in the hospital. Theo shakes his head 'no' at her looking like he is preparing for her to melt down as well. "Have you ever been forced to lay on the liquid remains of another person because they couldn't be bothered to clean the damn floor before replacing a fucking warm hole to stick their dicks in?" Again Theo just shakes his head at her. "How about this one, have you ever been suspended from the ceiling completely vulnerable to a group of people intent on seeing how-"

"Stop." Elsie whips her face over to Rhett and gapes at him. "I know you lived through it but the point you're trying to make is only proving that you need to see a shrink." His tone is even and calm but the slight emphasis on using her earlier phrasing hints at the fury buzzing around him. She blinks a few times before dropping her gaze to her lap. "It doesn't make you less to need help, Peaches." Rhett is squished in between me and her as he guides her face up to meet his gaze. I swallow and look away at their strangely intimate moment.

"Have you ever loved someone you shouldn't Mason?"She asks quietly like sweet secrets being exchanged by young lovers. I push down my jealousy manually with a hand over my stomach.

"Yes." He replies, loud and proud. I know he means her but damn I wish he didn't.

"I'm not *your* peaches anymore." She whispers lightly. I tense, there's an underlying implication that she just isn't his anymore - but that she feels she belongs to someone. And I have an idea of who that someone is. My gaze clashes with Theo's and he gives a slight tip of his head acknowledging he picked up on that too.

"I'm not *Mason* anymore either." He says with a smirk. "I'm Rhett." The tension breaks as they begin to chuckle and then we all dissolve into hysterics over his stupid line.

"How about we take the new TV for a test drive, hmm?" Theo interjects after we've settled some.

"Movie night?"Elsie whispers.

"Movie night." Rhett repeats louder as he nods.

"Burritos…?" She questions quietly. They both

look to me and I grin.

"Burritos." I confirm. They both dash off the couch like kids to begin gathering supplies.

"I'm more of a popcorn guy myself but I can get down with Mexican movie night." Theo shrugs as he seizes the remote and logs into various apps.

"Oh no. We'll still have popcorn and as much junk as I can order. We will be the burritos." I can't hide the amusement as he gapes at me.

"I'm not sure I know what you mean…" He states slowly. Right on time, Rhett and Elsie return with every blanket and pillow they can find giggling.

"Me first!" Rhett sings.

"No way! You're huge, it'd take all of us to get you rolled." Elsie argues. I can't help smiling as a feeling of familiarity settles over me watching them together. It's everything I've longed for since our lives exploded and my heart gives a little squeeze of appreciation.

Chapter 18

Elsie
Present Day

This evening with the guys makes my heart ache and long-forgotten feelings of freedom and love settle into me. Normalcy. Then I remember my parents are dead. Mason and Milo are now Rhett and Liam. Oh, and there is a fucking cop crashing our 'normal night' because danger lurks in every corner and crevice of this godforsaken earth. Danger that these guys know nothing about and cannot possibly keep me safe from. No, someone has to be in that lifestyle to know how to avoid it. Someone like Reaper.

Like me.

That thought flakes away any remaining warm and fuzzies as my gaze trails over the guys, massive lumps on the floor surrounded by junk food wrappers and empty soda cans. Mason has already broken out of his burrito and is splayed like a star while Miles is still tucked in neatly. Officer Belton is stretched out on the couch with a blanket half hazardly thrown over him. He was not interested in our antics and unsurprisingly no one even tried to pressure him into it. They all seem so calm and peaceful like there isn't horrid things happening all over the world right now as they rest. There is nothing 'normal' in this world anymore. It was always just a disguise in the first place to hide the true nature of humans. Familiar disgust coats my tongue. I don't belong here anymore.

I quietly slip off the couch and away from them and their delusions, their restful slumber and 'normal' lives. I pad silently over to the bookcase Reaper was moving around today. Knowing what I do of him, he has likely left me some kind of direction on how to find him. What his next steps will be. I need something, anything to cling to. He has been my anchor in this turbulent existence for too long.

I need him.

It doesn't take me long to see the paper folded and tucked tightly into a crack on the empty shelf. I tug at it, and it slides easily into my grip, a thrill of excitement sparking within me, making me grin. Just as I'm about to unfold it and discover what directions it might hold, I hear the rustle of movement behind me. I glance towards the guys, the atmosphere shifting ever so slightly, and catch Theo's gaze locked onto mine. His expression is a mix of curiosity and something else—something unreadable that makes my heart race just a bit faster. I can feel the weight of the moment, the anticipation hanging thick in the air, and for a heartbeat, I almost regret my choice. *Almost*.

"What are you doing?" He eyes me warily, his gaze finding the ntoe in my grasp. I hold it to my chest like the precious treasure it is and shake my head too frantically. "Ellie, what is that?" His voice raises and the other guys stir.

"N-nothing." I stammer nervously. The tone of my voice has Rhett sitting up with a pointed glare at Theo.

"Leave her alone. She can wander around her *home*." Rhett grumbles, shaking Liam roughly to rouse him as well. "Mr. Badge needs a hotel room."

"No, she's got something from that book shelf. The *empty* one." Theo argues indignantly. "Come here, what did you find?' He demands.

"Hey, man! Don't talk to her like that." Rhett rises and so does Theo and they dissolve into shouting nonsense insults at each other.

"Go to the room." Liam instructs as he trirs prying them apart. I don't hesitate, clutching the note like a life line as I flee to the back room. My heart pounds as I lean back against the closed door.

I can't stay here.

I hurriedly open the note from Reaper and breathe a sigh of relief - of course, he had a plan for me. I knew he still wanted me - no, he needs me. This means he needs me. I neatly fold it back up and rush to the closet where they had some of my new clothes placed. Slipping on jeans, a sweater and shoes I turn to the lone window in the room.

I try not to think about how far the fall is from the second story as I open it easily and lean over. For Reaper I'd do just about anything.

Including jumping out of a window - because he asked me to.

Taking a deep breathe I toss one leg out and momentarily reconsider, listening to Rhett and Liam defending my actions without so much as a single question. But no, I have to go. They can't protect me and I can't protect them. Reaper already knows where they live. The only hope they have for not just being murdered is if I go back and express to Reaper what they mean to me.

Without wasting another second I let myself fall, bending at my knees and rolling to absorb the shock I bite my lip hard to stifle the groan of pain. Nothing feels broken though so I move quickly to clear their field of vision when they ultimately realize I've run away.

Excitement courses through my veins and a smile

settles on my lip. I'm completely insane but maybe thats okay. Maybe Reaper will see me differently now. See me as a person instead of an object.

Yes, maybe this experience has helped him see *me*. Or maybe I finally see me again. A hysterical laugh bubbles up as I take in my true freedom. No one to tell me what to do or say or feel.

The further I walk, the more blissful I feel but there is a rage building in my heart. Who are Milo and Mason to decide my life for me? *Rhett and Liam,* I mentally roll my eyes at the faint reminder of how their lives have changed too. I don't care. What do they know of me anymore? And Officer Belton can screw off, he is just collecting a paycheck and using me to fuel his hero complex. Even Reaper is just telling me what to do and who to be - without even considering what I want! None of them are thinking about what I actually want. Rage boils under my skin now, brimming with ideas for revenge.

Fuck all of them.

Chapter 19

I am not a patient man. She will come. She does not love them. No, my Peach is just as twisted and obsessed as I am. I knew it the moment I swept her out of that horrid hostel in Atlanta. My twisted little Peach would learn not just to obey me, but love me. Become so obsessed with me that she'd rationalize all the physical pain I had to put her through to teach her. To better her. Yes, she'd understand.

The dying fluorescent lighting and dripping of a leaky pipe somewhere far inside this dank warehouse makes me feel slightly frazzled. I much prefer the clean, static silence or swanky style of the life I've built for Peach and I.

She must be feeling overwhelmed herself. What if she gets lost? Or worse, decides not to come at all?

No, she will. She has to. Or I will kill them all just

to prove to her how much I adore her. I love her.

I *love* her.

That realization had slapped me with an uncage-able fire when I'd seen them take her from me. Some-one had squealed - dropped the ball on protecting what is mine. SO I killed them all. Every person who knew about that fucking shipping container expired at my hands. Including pretty police boys old partner - funny how he seems so unphased by the disappearance of that dirty little rat. Perhaps they didn't gt along. Or maybe he was too focused on playing house with my Peach to pick up the phone call from his chief.

Still, it was far too easy to find them all anyway. Even easier to kill one of those workers and enter their home. God, just seeing her standing there in her stupid pale pink sweatsuit had set my body a blaze. I had missed her. I still miss her. I will until I have her sweet form against mine. The creak of the door has me glancing up, a small smile playing on my face as I stroke my pistol in my lap.

She is truly hypnotic.

And, *mine.*

About the Author

Happily married to her high school sweetheart, Tullie Summer's life has been akin to many of the romance novels we all long for with just enough tragedy and struggle to keep the pages turning. Previously a model, child actor, professional dancer and instructor creating has always been a large part of her life but as time presented new challenges, she had to shift her focus to more sedentary outlets for her creativity and thus an impassioned author was born from this obsessive reader. With the support of her husband and two children, she became a self-published author in 2023 featuring Street Lit and several Kindle Vella productions. She loves spending her days painting, baking and enjoying picnics, usually with a book in hand. She spins stories of love, loss and never guarantees a happy ending.

Keep an eye out for her first full length novel, releasing summer 2024!

Join her email list for more updates.

Also by Tullie Summers

Street Lit

In 45-minutes or less, this short story will show you a rollercoaster of a love story that will leave you wanting more.

Emmett is burnt out after over-working himself in hopes of providing for his parents and needs something or someone to bring joy back into his days. Heaven is still haunted by the choices in her past but turns out to be exactly what Emmett needs. Delighted by each other their love comes easy - but life is never that simple, is it?